"You saw the killer?"

Concern reduced Cole's voice to a hoarse whisper. "Did he hurt you?"

Kate shook her head. "I didn't see him. He left the note in my house." She hesitated. "This is the second communication I've had from him."

"Why didn't you tell me? This scares the hell out of me. If you were wise, you'd be frightened, too."

"Maybe it'll feed your ego to know that for a few minutes, I *was* scared. But if you're wanting me to cave in and be a proper lady—I can't."

"That's a crock," Cole snapped. "That you're a woman has nothing to do with anything. I've worked with plenty of women."

Kate took a deep, bracing breath. "But you don't sleep with them, do you, Chief?"

Dear Reader,

The verdict is in: legal thrillers are a hit. And in response to this popular demand, we give you the first of Harlequin Intrigue's ongoing "Legal Thrillers."

In this new program we'll be bringing you some of your favorite stories. Stories of secret scandals and crimes of passion. Of legal eagles who battle the system . . . and undeniable desire.

Look for the "Legal Thriller" flash for the best in suspense!

Sincerely,

Debra Matteucci
Senior Editor & Editorial Coordinator
Harlequin Books
300 E. 42nd St.
New York, NY 10017

Within the Law

Laraine McDaniel

Harlequin Books

TORONTO • NEW YORK • LONDON
AMSTERDAM • PARIS • SYDNEY • HAMBURG
STOCKHOLM • ATHENS • TOKYO • MILAN
MADRID • WARSAW • BUDAPEST • AUCKLAND

For my sister Carol, with love

ISBN 0-373-22272-6

WITHIN THE LAW

This edition published by arrangement with Harlequin Enterprises B. V.

Printed in U.S.A.

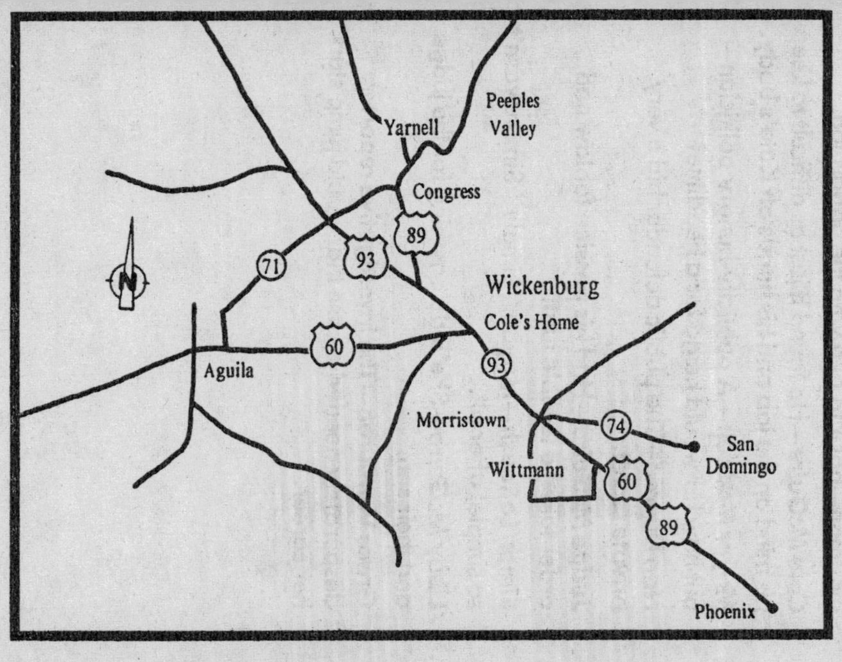
Peeples
Valley
Yarnell
Congress
89
93
71
N
Wickenburg
Cole's Home
60
Aguila
93
Morristown
74
San
Domingo
Wittmann
60
89
Phoenix

CAST OF CHARACTERS

Kate Quin—Her job was to climb into the mind of a madman—not into bed with the opposition.

Cole McGuire—He found it just as difficult to keep his mind on the job and his hands off Kate's body.

Mayor Madden—A publicity-hungry politician—but how far would he go for a headline?

Nan Dupree—The public defender hid a very private secret.

Judge McGuire—Had his passion for law and order taken a terrible turn?

Simon LaRoush—Maybe "Simple" Simon wasn't so simple, after all.

Libby McGuire—She'd do anything for the judge and their son.

Grace VanBuren—The investigative reporter desperately needed a case that would jump start her career.

Chapter One

FBI agent Kate Quin had neither eaten nor slept during the flight from Quantico to Phoenix—her method for defeating jet lag. She had been five hours in the air, chasing a sun about to burn itself out on the western horizon. The recycled air inside the 727 cabin had turned heavy and stale. She squeezed her eyes shut and kneaded her temples.

Can you catch him? the San Domingo city mayor had asked, as though she were about to engage in a footrace. It was an appalling question....

Kate didn't fool herself. Failure was the chief hazard of her occupation. She was a psychological profiler, trained to classify the behavior of madmen. She took pains not to exaggerate the success rate.

That's up to chance, she'd answered truthfully. There had been little else to say. She'd felt so insignificant against the odds.

The plane reduced cruising speed to begin its descent, creating the eerie sensation that it was standing still and might fall from the sky at any moment. Kate sat motionless, her gaze fixed on the most recent crime-scene photographs. How this latest killer operated could be much more revealing than why he committed the heinous acts. Kate thought about that. Behavioral analysis was based on the assumption that there was some kind of interaction between the offender and the victim. There had been three victims so far, and she had yet to establish a relationship.

What the killer had done with this victim after death, was obvious. Postmortem ligature marks around the neck emerged as the most glaring aspect of the case: the killer had hung the corpse.

Categorizing him as crazy was grossly inadequate. Kate knew he was so much more. *But what else?*

Several seconds passed while she studied the pictures. She concentrated on the victim. What had the killer seen? Before the hanging? Before the fatal gunshot wound? *He saw his victim weak and vulnerable. Was he mad at the victim for dying?*

She sank back in her seat and fought down the flat feeling that made her feel helpless, inconsequential, as if she were being pressed like a nasty insect between glass.

It struck her again how meager this last victim's existence had been. There was a history of petty crimes. Another thing the decedents had in common. Their masculine gender had Kate wondering if these heinous acts were hate crimes against men.

There were no indications of a struggle. Had the victim begged to be spared? Kate could see his fear with sickening vividness, giving pleasure to the murderer, incapacitating the victim. Why hadn't the victim fought back? With no signs of restraint evident, familiarity remained a possibility.

What else? No signs of panic. Though the killer took great risks in attacking during the day, he had remained coolly in control, deliberating and improvising as he went along. He had systematically murdered in cold blood, then made use of his "postmortem kit" of toiletries, facial tissues and hanging rope.

This morbid consideration shown the corpse unnerved Kate. The idea of respect would not occur readily to a sociopath. *Why did he clean up the body?* As a symbolic act? To conceal the postmortem mutilation?The preliminary autopsy report was unclear about whether animals had inflicted the injuries, or whether the subsequent wounds had drawn the animals.

As she sat, cramped and fatigued, a certainty came over Kate. As surely as he killed, the murderer consciously left behind clues. Because he dared to. *He wanted her to know why.* That was important to him. He was evil, but never stupid, never apathetic.

Kate suddenly felt too warm and wanted to pull off her jacket, but knew the holster she wore would attract attention. She didn't want curious eyes aimed at her.

This killer was a psychopath—a maniac—but he was much, much more, whoever he was, and he was worth knowing, if only to Kate. Exhilaration nudged her closer to the limits of self-control, because she knew he was waiting to meet her, too.

"American Air, flight 512, is cleared to land in Phoenix. Please fasten..."

The flight attendant's voice silenced her thoughts. Kate sprang forward in her seat, her damp blouse pressed cold against her back. The cabin felt too warm. She aimed the overhead vent at her face, allowing the rush of cool air to dry the sweat beading across her forehead. The plane banked to make its final approach into Sky Harbor airport, and Kate pressed herself deeper into the safety of her seat.

The landing gear bounced off the runway once, twice, then went into the squealing skid necessary to halt the speeding hunk of metal. Kate had hated flying even before her parents were lost in a fiery air crash. Planes had always made her feel vulnerable.

Cole McGuire made her feel vulnerable, too. He had loved her. She had no doubt about that. But he'd ended what they'd started. The realization overwhelmed her. *We should see other people,* he'd said, and the hurting had begun.

So why had she returned? Curiosity? Or a perverse desire to tempt fate? She was here to show San Domingo Police Chief Cole McGuire how to do his job. He wouldn't be too happy about that.

COLE MCGUIRE HAD prayed for this moment. He wasn't quite sure, now that it had arrived, what he should do or say. Terrifying hope gripped him. He considered bolting. But he was no longer a desperate boy, needing a miracle, continually searching for it in the faces of foster parents, finding disappointment instead. Libby and the Judge had ended all of that for him by investing their life in a difficult nine-year-old.

"Cole?"

The collapse of all his defenses came with the gentle sound of Kate's voice. While her luminous mahogany eyes offered only a fragile embrace, her husky voice enveloped him, caressed him, reminding him of intimacies once shared.

"You don't look like a federal investigator," he murmured.

As he spoke, Cole met her gaze, and slowly, he began to feel alive again, in a way he had not experienced since daring fate to take Kate from him. Slowly, too, he began to take stock of what was happening.

Because something *was* happening.

For a moment he was unsure, almost afraid to think about it, to pin it down too closely. Then an inexplicable calm settled over him and he knew. In one fleeting but crucial instant, Cole realized he'd been granted a second chance.

No decision was necessary. He knew he was going to act. He was determined not to let this chance slip away.

"What do they look like," Kate was asking, "these federal investigators?"

"Definitely not as good as you do." His gaze traveled down the length of her and back. He smiled with pressed lips. "You'll need shoes if you plan to work with me,'' he said, making a gallant attempt at non-chalance.

They stared at each other again, brown eyes locking with blue. Kate glanced away first, seemingly distracted by her bare feet. But she had never been concerned about what other people thought of her. Even now she was laughing, tossing her head. He loved the way she did that, unintentionally showing him her perfect profile. The pulse in her throat was throbbing.... He could almost feel it. Missing her for eighteen long months had enabled him to do that. Though they stood within inches of each other, they were still miles apart. Cole instinctively knew he would need to make the leap of his life.

''You have a strange way of saying hello,'' she said softly, warming him with a sincere smile.

Until now, he'd been joining the dots, building on the present, hoping sheer momentum would carry him forward from one point to the next. He gave serious consideration to the impulse demanding that he advance another step and pull her into his arms.

''This is awkward,'' he said instead, the hope in his voice unmistakable as he searched her expression for a sign.

''I'm sorry.''

The cloud cover of pain shading her eyes hurt him. He waved her apology away and said, ''I'm not blaming you. How's life been treating you?'' He felt ridiculous for asking it, but her answer was quick and assured.

"It's had ups and downs, but basically good." She rushed ahead. "I've given this a lot of thought...and I think you should know up front..."

His heart sank. His breath hitched. Something in her tone filled him with regret, disappointment, guilt.

"I want this to work—" She plowed on, the words bumping into each other. He breathed easily again. "I'm not talking about us." His heart went down for a second time. "I think we can get past the important things standing in our way. I'm very organized—you're not. I speak before I think. You tend to be critical. S-stuff like that," she stammered. "What do you think?"

"Depends. I'm a realist, remember?" He could almost hear the whir of Kate's brain recording his answer just before she tossed her response at him.

"What does that mean?"

"I thought you'd sold out to the enemy."

"I was hoping to avoid these interagency squabbles," she said, her bluntness not without charm. "Sometimes they take weird turns, delay investigations. All I want is to provide you with an accurate sketch of this madman's mind."

"Right," he mumbled, his tone belying anything close to what he was thinking and feeling. He could feel the tips of his ears burning. His temper was up. "Let me remind you that it was the mayor who called in the FBI. Me? I'm not sold on the merits of a psychological diagnosis of the killer's mental disorders.

"Frankly," he added, "I don't see where you can tell me anything." He knew she would try. She was bright, but it was overachieving that always drove her to the head of the class.

"All your psychological explanations for why he's committing these murders sound intriguing," he continued, "and I'll grant you, relying on police procedure is far less interesting. But I'm a conservative cop, and that makes me suspicious of using mental-health profiling to catch criminals." Dammit. A trickle of frustration had found its way into his words. He cut it off, because it was dangerous to risk further comment.

"I may not be able to offer anything new to the investigation," she admitted, "other than a helping hand to keep you on course."

Watch your step. Maybe she hadn't uttered those precise words, but he'd heard the warning, nonetheless. She'd managed to slap him down a notch without lifting a hand. Cole drew a breath while he did some hard and fast thinking.

"Fair enough," he capitulated.

His yearning for her intensified. As surely as if his lips were on her skin, he could remember loving the taste of her body, one summer night in San Domingo.

"I've got to admit," she said, "under the circumstances, you seem relaxed. The job used to eat you up."

That was as close to the past, *their* past, as she had dared to venture. That suited him for the time being, because he was too shaken by her nearness, and by the fact that after eighteen months of nothing, he could instantly reclaim the urge to make love to her until neither of them could move. *Funny,* Cole thought, *how little time changes things.*

"I still work under a mayor who hates my guts. I've got a city under siege. The list of wannabe serial killers grows longer every day." He looked at her. "Now? I couldn't care less."

"Not to worry, huh? You've mellowed?"

"I don't think that's it. Maybe I've gotten a little smarter. Don't bang my head against walls for the hell of it anymore."

He felt a grin playing on his mouth. Kate smiled back. To him, she no longer appeared tense. Her delicate face was both sensitive and intelligent, oval in shape, more striking now that she wore her dark hair so short. Her row of bangs matched the color of her arresting eyes, intensifying them.

"Charming," she said in the soft voice he knew so well.

"Definitely charming," he murmured, in the most beguiling tone he could produce.

Her body was much thinner, more athletic looking. His eyes roamed freely, finally coming to rest on her makeup-free face again, where variegated light played across her sun-pinkened cheeks. Cole wanted to seize her, hold her against him, but it was time to attend to more pressing matters. "What's on your agenda now?"

"I've got an appointment with the mayor," she said. "Care to join me?"

"I don't think so, but I'll drop you. If you're not going to be long—"

"Just long enough to introduce myself and let him know I'm in town."

"I'll be back for you."

Kate's eyes narrowed and her jaw tightened.

"What's wrong?" he pressed, unwilling to let her slip away, even if it meant taking on the mayor. "I told you I'll be there. Trust me."

"I'll have to," she said. "That's the problem."

COLE LOOKED FIT AND as handsome as ever. Cole, the only man she knew who refused to stiffen under a white shirt and tie.

Maybe the fact that he was a cop explained his look of solid strength, his square-jawed, dependable aura. His camel-colored slacks blended with his deeply tanned body. The familiar dark brown leather jacket, shiny from wear, hid much of his build, but she could see that he was still broad-chested, wide through the shoulders, and lean in the hips.

"Let's get out of here," he said. "Give me your shoes and I'll slip them on for you."

Kate focused on her feet. Murphy's Law? Or Cole McGuire's Law? So much for her designer suit. She had smacked down a month's wages for the outfit. She handed him the high heels. His mouth twitched at one corner as he eyed the expensive shoes, and she knew he was amused.

She admired his physique as he folded himself into a kneeling position. She leaned against his solid shoulders to steady herself, expecting meltdown to occur any second. Cole was strong and lean and on the plus side of six feet tall. He'd been a powerful bed partner.

He took hold of Kate's foot, transporting her to another time, another place...where she could feel his fingertips caressing the length of her naked body, skimming, touching, skimming, brushing her thigh....

With his hands on her, thinking straight became difficult. Sensations inside her collided...sparking a fire ready to blaze to life. The familiar smell of his after-shave, faint but evocative, drifted over her. For months she'd told herself she'd imagined that scent, but she hadn't. It was as real as the man at her feet. She was moist and embarrassed because of it.

She remembered all of it...every delicious detail.... The next moment, she was trying to banish the memory of his mouth on hers...the weight of his body when it covered her own....

"Can you walk in those things?" he asked as he stood upright, nodding at the nearly three-inch heels. "If you can't keep up, I'll have to leave you behind."

He grinned at her. But Kate fielded that one, letting her hands slide from his shoulders. "Threats are part of the territory, Chief." The developing smile twinkled with amusement. "I'll manage both—the shoes and the threat."

He caught her eye and grinned again, then his gaze traveled the length of her approvingly. She'd definitely made an impression with the shoes.

"You always did have terrific legs."

"Forget it, McGuire."

"Come on. We should already be rolling. I understand you're the best," he said over his shoulder.

"I'm proud of my record with the Bureau," she replied, trying to sound casual. "I didn't think I'd last a month there, you want to know the truth."

They had reached the elevators by the time Kate remembered the rest of her luggage—a bag she had checked.

"What is it?" Cole asked.

"One suitcase—"

"Give me your claim check and wait here. While I'm gone, figure out another pair of shoes to wear. We've got a long night ahead of us."

Kate watched him until he disappeared, drinking in the sight of him. Bolder than a magician, he had walked right up to her and reached for her heart, using a brilliant piece of magic. That he could still cast his spell over her, hurt nearly as much as the sharp pain of his betrayal. She would have to watch him, because she knew—she damned well knew—that illusionists needed watching.

If hearing herself paged to a white phone in the Sky Harbor terminal surprised Kate, seeing Judge McGuire emerge from one of the elevators proved even more startling. She'd been too excited to pay much attention to the whir of the elevator, so much so that when Cole's father emerged, he caught her completely off guard.

"Welcome home, Kate."

The sight of him brightened her spirits.

"I wasn't expecting you, but I'm glad you're here," she said sincerely.

The Judge slipped his arms around her, and she fell against him like a child who had just been rescued from a dreadful experience. At once, she drew back to have a solid look at her old friend and mentor.

It was obvious that the stringent schedule imposed on the superior-court jurist was taking its toll. This was one of those rare occasions when the fastidious dresser was without his suit coat and the crisply ironed white shirt did little or nothing to disguise his hunched shoulders.

"Did you have me paged?" Kate asked.

"I was afraid I'd miss you. It's six-thirty. I knew your flight arrived at six." He scanned the area. "Is Cole here?" he asked, casting dark, liquid brown eyes upon her, the intense gaze reminding her of her father.

His solemn expression frightened most people, but she had always taken comfort in his steady, serious countenance. She grinned and nodded. "He's collecting my luggage."

The Judge bobbed his head in acknowledgement, and the corners of his eyes crinkled as he grinned. Lovingly, he patted her cheek with one of his gnarled hands. The once-lean, nicely balanced body now appeared too thin and lanky. Still, there was a wiry strength about him. He looked as though sleep had been eluding him. His eyelids were puffy and hooded.

"Where are your glasses?" she asked, surprised he would be without them.

"I was securing a new wren feeder to a Palo Verde branch this morning, when the ladder fell against the tree. I took a nasty scrape. Broke my glasses."

"Where's your spare pair?"

"I was wearing them," he said wryly. His eyes twinkled. "You won't tell Libby I was on the ladder?" He pressed his finger to his lips to signal silence.

"Why, Judge, frankly I'm shocked."

"You know how she worries."

Kate nodded before she could stop herself. She doubted if she would ever possess the rock-solid loyalty Libby McGuire demonstrated toward her family. She doted on Cole. When he moved into an apartment in town, she focused her attention on the Judge. She could hear Libby's voice still—*There's no law against caring about the ones you love.*

Kate had been a recipient of that overflow of love even more so when her parents were killed. She would never forget Libby's steady hands holding her the endless times she awoke, screaming, from a nightmare, or forget Libby's deep voice soothing her in the dead of night.

"All right," Kate supplied finally. "But you're incorrigible. You know that, don't you?"

"Blame it on the deer. After dining decadently on birdseed, they found dessert in Libby's flower garden. So, you see, I only had her tea roses at heart."

"How is Libby?" Kate asked while her mind's eye conjured a mental image of Cole's robust mother tending her elaborate garden.

From Libby, Kate had learned to appreciate what hard work could achieve. Her rose garden sprang off the side of a craggy hill like a phoenix.

"She wanted so to be here to meet you," he said, his expressive eyes widening, "but I came right from the courthouse." He paused. It was rare for him not to come directly to the point. "You didn't answer our letter. We want you to stay with us in Wickenburg, in the guesthouse. What do you say?"

"Thank you," she said, pressing her lips together to hold back the lump building in her throat.

She'd missed them so. The McGuires had been there for her when she'd needed them most. Libby. The Judge. And Cole.

"You've made us very happy with this visit. Having you here again is a treat for us. And for Cole, too, you know."

Kate couldn't define the situation between her and Cole. She didn't want to speculate, either. But there *was* something.... He still had that power. Ridiculous, but true.

"Yes... Well, we have a job to do."

His brow furrowed. "Yes. You've had the misfortune to arrive right in the middle of something dreadful. I know you chose this job, but it still seems a gruesome task." He sighed. "Well, I parked in a reserved spot.'' He patted her on the forearm in a paternal gesture. ''I must hurry.''

''Don't you want to wait for Cole?''

''No, no, don't even bother to tell him I was here. I just wanted to make sure you were met at the airport. Just like old times, huh, Kate?''

She smiled gently, belying what was really going on in her mind. *Wait!* she wanted to call out. *He betrayed me, dammit. I wanted commitment. I got freedom....* I'm *the victim here....*

Nothing short of a magic act would put the pieces from the past back together. And no amount of magic could change her mind about that.

Chapter Two

Like magic, steam rose from the coffee, snaking and creating the illusion that a genie was about to appear to grant the usual three wishes. But Cole had only one: a second chance with Kate. Nothing short of magic would give him the power to reenter her world.

"You gave me a start," Kate said almost breathlessly, as if he had surprised her by returning.

"You changed shoes." He surveyed her sneakers.

"Good of you to notice."

"I noticed," he murmured, his gaze still dancing over her legs. "Let's get out of here."

She remained quiet for the duration of the elevator ride to the rooftop parking area. When they reached his battered Caprice sedan, she still hadn't spoken.

"You're very quiet," she said.

"Me?"

"What's on your mind?"

"Already trying to divine my thoughts?" he challenged. "Or whatever it is that you do?"

"You make it sound as if I read tea leaves."

"Just don't expect me to get excited about your mind games. I'm not into dissecting psychos," he said. "I don't give a damn about his psyche."

"Sounds reasonable," she said mildly, not the least bit unnerved that he had too bluntly overstated his opinion of her purpose here.

Too late to apologize, he said instead, "This one's a monster—who deserves to be punished."

"Punished?"

"That's my job, Kate," he said, moving around the car to unlock the door for her. "You're the fixer." His cool facade was neatly in place. "But you might want to rethink slicing open the brain of a madman like this one."

"Now I'm dissecting frogs?" she said. "My work is a bit more challenging than that."

"Maybe it's the challenge you're after." Cole cocked his head slightly and looked thoughtful.

"We're all after the challenge."

"This one's different. There's a dangerous playground inside his head. Watch your step there, Kate."

He pulled open the passenger door, then walked around to the driver's side of the car.

"And you'll see to it that I do?"

"We could spend a lot of time on this—"

"On what?"

"Looking for people you've invented. Right up front, understand that I'll be calling the shots."

She inhaled slowly, allowing herself a few extra seconds to collect her poise. She summoned a tight little smile, then spoke deliberately.

"If that makes you feel safe, go ahead. But understand this. We can work together, or we can work apart, in which case I'll be five minutes behind your every step."

He leaned against the car, rested his arms on its roof, and stared across at her. The chilly air held a bite. The only sound was the pervasive hum of slow-moving automobiles looking for parking spots. He sucked in a deep breath—something he did just before he turned to instinct.

"Are you involved?" he asked casually, attempting to conceal the way pain flattened his tone.

The reaction that passed over her features was quite the opposite of what he expected. It wasn't defensiveness or guilt or sadness. It was as close to fury as anything he'd ever seen in Kate's expression. He hadn't meant to go quite that far. But now that he had, there was no turning back.

She disappeared into the passenger side of the sedan. Cole rested his head on the roof of the car, squeezed his eyes shut briefly. Feeling momentarily off-balance, he straightened, pushed a hand through his hair, then slid into the driver's seat.

He dared more than just a glance at her. His hand simply went to her, to trace the outline of her mouth with a finger. Automatically, her lips parted. She stared up at him for a moment, sending his self-control running wild. Sensations shook him as he traced the contours of her chin, her lips. The look in her eyes acknowledged that he knew every inch of her body. He did. Intimately.

"You didn't ask if *I* was involved," he murmured.

"No," she said, shaking her head. "I didn't."

Disappointment descended on cue. But it was the hope that clutched at his gut as he sat humbly by, waiting, praying for a miracle.

KATE NEEDED TO KNOW. But that need was eroding all that was left of her pride. Silently she drew in a long breath to restore her resolve. They drove in silence to the San Domingo city complex.

When Cole eased the car into a parking space, she was still fighting for the control to speak calmly.

"Kate, we need to talk," he said before she could get a word out.

"That's why I'm here, Cole," she replied, wisely keeping her expression blank.

He could talk until his tongue fell out. The old rage was burning inside her as she exited the Caprice. Outside the car, she leaned down to look at him through the passenger-side window.

"I'll need fifteen minutes," she told him.

"I'll be back."

There was nothing else to say. Kate straightened and turned to leave. She managed to cover the brief distance into the mayor's office without looking back.

SAN DOMINGO MAYOR MADDEN wanted to field this one personally. Kate's orders were to report directly to him.

The door to his office stood wide open. Nan Dupree was already in the mayor's office when Kate stepped into the waiting area outside it. She had recognized Nan at once. The public defender was one of those lanky, attractive blondes, the high-strung thoroughbred type. Today her perfect hair and makeup were offset by her nervousness. There was no mistaking the look in her eyes—pure panic. Her gaze jerked from side to side, searching the paneled walls of the mayor's office like a trapped animal inspecting the bars of its cage.

Through the open door, Kate could hear the sound of Nan's low, angry mumbling, and then her voice rising above the mayor's as she turned her wrath on Simon LaRoush, a pasty-faced little man with the look of a reptile. His small black eyes almost never blinked, but his nervous tongue constantly darted out to wet his veal-colored lips. Kate had sat in on his hearings often while attending law school.

"This kind of indiscretion has got to stop!" the mayor said to the two counselors.

The mayor's temper was up. He rolled his shoulders and rubbed his face with the palms of his two thick paws. Nan was crying softly now.

"You can't seriously subscribe to those rumors," Simon said incredulously. "Judge McGuire is the one—"

"Dammit, Simon, you're the prosecuting attorney. You know their impact has nothing to do with validity—put a stop to them."

"They're an indictment against my integrity. I view this as attorney bashing—"

"Did you assume you could blow me off this easily?" The mayor clicked his tongue in disgust. "You assumed too much."

"You going to back me on this, Nan?" Simon demanded. "You want to tell the mayor what's *really* going on here?"

"Shut up, Simon," she snapped, tears drying with the heat of her anger. "Just what are you trying to imply?"

"You know exactly what I'm saying."

Nan looked to the mayor and pointed a finger at Simon. "And you believe *him?*" She laughed mirthlessly, her fingers raking frantically through her hair. She was about to break. Kate recognized the signs.

"It doesn't matter," Nan said without waiting for a response. "I came in here to resign."

The mayor's face mottled into various shades of red. "Are you nuts? You can't resign!"

"Watch me!"

Nan bolted from the office, with Simon in hot pursuit. Kate stepped out of her way, but not without nodding a polite hello when the defense attorney caught her breath and looked at her, startled. Resentment replaced Nan's broken, weary look, and she vanished through the door that led to the main lobby. Without acknowledging Kate, either, Simon followed.

The mayor pressed his fleshy body against his desk, staring suspiciously as Kate approached him.

"I didn't know anyone was waiting," Madden said shortly.

"Kate Quin," she said, extending her hand. She was standing in the middle of his office, waiting to be offered a seat. She dropped her outstretched hand and continued. "We did have an appointment?" Kate asked.

The mayor's face was about as animated as a graveyard headstone. He grunted an impersonal greeting, then turned his back to her as he stepped toward his desk. There was nothing remarkable about him, save his six-foot-plus height, swanlike neck, and bulging eyes that reminded Kate of an exotic fish. He sat down and cut straight to the bone.

"We've got ourselves another mess that's gonna send shock waves clear to the Gulf of Mexico and back."

What happened to "Welcome to San Domingo," or "How was the flight?" or "Need a ride?" Kate wondered.

"That's why I'm here," she said, struggling to keep her tone compliant, cooperative. "Why not give Chief McGuire and me a chance to set up a task force?"

The mayor performed a nervous ritual with his clothes: adjusting a perfectly knotted tie, inspecting his jacket for lint, then adjusting the tie again.

"There's no doubt in my mind that McGuire and his people can conduct a competent investigation, but I want someone on this job who I know can hit a curve."

A *curve?*

"I steer clear of the politics," Kate said.

"It's no secret that I don't get on with McGuire. That's why I sent for you. McGuire's attitude makes for undue friction. I don't like it."

"Attitude?"

"Damn right! He's a loner. And I need a team player."

"Chief McGuire has a masters degree in criminal justice from the University of Tucson." The mayor merely clicked his tongue and wagged his head in disgust. "His 'friction,'" Kate continued, "might save the city a lot of embarrassment."

"I still don't like it," the mayor muttered. "You keep him on a short leash. I'm calling the shots here."

Twice during the same evening she'd been told that. Was it something in the water?

"Right," Kate murmured.

Just when I thought you were beginning to like me.

The mayor considered himself a political animal; Kate regarded the man as tourist minded; either way, if they didn't find a perp fast, fallout from the "mess," as Madden put it, would cover Cole up to his knees.

"Care to hazard a guess about what's going on with this psycho?" he asked.

Kate rubbed her temple. She needed aspirin and caffeine to do battle with what was mounting into a five-alarm headache.

"I have given it some thought," she muttered. "He displays an intense need to punish."

Her revelation was followed by a dramatic pause while the mayor allowed the ambiguous disclosure to hang on the air.

"Well, well, very good. And how does this point us to the killer? You think someone is trying to eradicate all the deadbeats in the city?" Deep belly laughter. "That's not all bad, Agent."

"It's reasonable to entertain the possibility that someone is inflicting punishment by means of eradication." Another pause. "You would have to read through the case files—"

"Don't condescend, Agent Quin."

"I'm concerned about his escalating need—"

"You're making a provisional assumption," he snapped. "That could be hazardous to my position."

"I wouldn't want to step on any toes."

"Yes, let's watch whose toes we step on, eh?"

Annoyed with the dismissal, Kate shot a disgusted look at the mayor. Then, not because she had given in, but because there was nothing else to say, she turned and left.

THE FEAR THAT THE killer would never slip up dominated Cole's existence—until a few moments ago when his chief detective had given him news that just might jump-start the flimsy investigation. He wanted to applaud as he watched Kate approaching the car from behind.

"You look like you could use some good news," he murmured as she slid onto the front seat.

"Desperately."

He started the engine, backed out of the space, eased into the flow of traffic.

"There's been a new development in the case."

Her face remained impassive, but he saw her breath catch. The revelation had startled her.

"The fourth victim went down shortly after five o'clock this afternoon—inside the San Domingo superior court."

"You took your time telling me." Kate sat in silence, waiting for him to provide information.

"Think this could be the work of a copycat?" he asked.

Kate rejected the idea. "A copycat would have picked a safer site, someplace where bringing in a gun wouldn't have been a problem."

"Visits to superior court are by invitation only," he muttered. "No drop-ins."

From the corner of his eye, he saw her bite her lower lip, then release it. "We'll want to eliminate the possibility of an insider."

"That shouldn't be a problem."

"Possible witnesses?" she asked.

Cole shook his head.

"Who made the 911 call?"

"There were two 911 calls."

"That carries a host of implications." He could see she was rapidly processing and storing the information. "I'll want the voice tapes compared to the call-ins from the killer. Also, times and caller identification—the origination locations."

"I'm already working on a match to the first three voice tapes reporting victim locations." He slowed the car to look directly into her eyes. "You up to another social call?"

Kate regarded him with suspicion.

"The victim's alive," he said shortly. "Just barely. In critical condition, with a .38 slug to the brain."

Her reaction was swift but quiet, coming only from her huge brown eyes, which had suddenly grown larger. "Any other inconsistencies?"

He looked across the seat at her. "A big one. The victim is a *woman*."

Chapter Three

"You really know how to play it for all it's worth," Kate said calmly enough, but he could see the light in her eyes. "Is the victim talking?"

"We're about to find out."

It was nine-twenty when they turned north onto Third Avenue. Cole could see the blue-and-red lights a block away. A uniformed officer met them at the entrance to the hospital parking garage.

"Great night to catch a psycho, Chief."

Cole raised his fist with one thumb up to the officer. The uniformed man grinned and nodded his approval, and Cole drove past him in search of a parking space.

"This is likely to get ugly," he said, looking at her from across the seat, feeling protective. He spoke again, his tone gentle. "Unless you like seeing yourself on the late-night news, it might be best, for the time being, for you to keep a low profile."

"I'm not a contagious disease," she objected. "I'm

an FBI agent—here to do a job—whether you appreciate that fact or not."

"Whoa." Cole pushed the air with the palm of his hand. "I was only thinking of you, Kate. I remember how the press treated you after your folks died."

Cole had a good idea how Kate felt about the media. Reporters had inundated her with questions when her parents had died in a plane wreck, and Kate had rightfully resented dealing with their insensitivity. For a moment he thought about the losses that had gone into the making of Kate. Dual degrees in psychology and law. A degree of something—admiration? respect?—filled him.

"Your presence will be viewed as validation that San Domingo has its first serial killer."

Her expression softened, and her tone relaxed. "I don't know for certain yet that we're dealing with a serial killer," she reminded him.

He arched a brow. "I thought you said four was the magic number."

Gunshot wounds were tricky. The victim had taken an injection of lead to the cranium, just below the left ear. He held out little hope for a miracle.

"Lots of things are possible, but we've got 3.5 victims," she corrected.

"What kind of a psycho do we have on our hands?"

"It's too early for labels."

"Everyone's a little crazy, is that it?"

"This one's experiencing a growing state of desperation, and that's what concerns me the most. This whole business makes great news. It's spectacle," she cautioned. "We've got to hold back something that will allow us to identify him if he tries to make contact with us."

She was quick; he'd always admired that about her.

"We've managed to hold back that he tidies up the corpses," he said finally. He gave her an enigmatic look. "Why do you do this sort of thing, Kate? You like getting inside their heads?"

"It's what I'm trained to do." She hesitated a moment. "This one's very ill."

Cole shrugged off a laugh. "You always were a fixer."

"When you read my profile, you'll understand the pain he's in."

Cole pulled into a parking space marked Reserved, and turned off the engine. He made no move to get out.

"I reserve my compassion for the victims and their families." His voice was cool, in control. "There's never enough to go around."

"I know," she said, reaching out to touch his arm.

She had done it unconsciously, instinctively. Still, deep down inside, something came to life inside him. With any encouragement, he would have pulled her into his arms where she belonged. But the fact was, Cole could take comfort in Kate's mere presence. He took hold of her hand and gently caressed, turned it palm side up to examine it, as though he might find answers there. Answers to how he was going to find his way back into Kate's life.

"How can you bleed over him?" he asked. "He's a monster."

"Try and understand that he feels the same despair as the families of his victims—that's why he kills."

"Does he feel what his victims feel when they're gasping for their last breath—pleading to be spared?"

"I don't know that." Her stubbornness was back.

"But you'd like to know."

"Yes," she answered honestly. He could feel the heat from her gaze burning a hole in him. "I'd like to know."

A soft smile parted her lush and beautiful lips. He should have opened the car door and got out, but the temptation to sit there and just watch her breathe, was more than he could bear.

"Kate...what are you doing here?" he asked, a bewildered note in his tone. "Doesn't it affect you?"

She withdrew her hand, and Cole had her answer.

He moved toward her then, eating up the distance separating them. Her face was in shadow, her eyes unreadable, but the power that his body held over hers was still there. He couldn't see the sparks, but he felt them, and lifted his hands to grip her shoulders. He was so close to her that he could feel her warm breath on his mouth. He should have resisted, but it was far too late to pull back now.

"Kate...Kate..." he murmured.

She met his hungry mouth so completely with her own that he wasn't sure which of them allowed the groan to escape. He pressed his lips against hers, and felt an awakening in his gut that made his entire body go on red alert. Her arms pulled him closer and she clung to him, her fingers feverishly massaging the small of his back.

His tongue darted at first, then slowly caressed every inch of her mouth, until the act became pure torture. Even as he withdrew, he realized the urgent need would surface again, and self-control was dwindling.

"I'm sorry for that," he mumbled, his words thick, his breathing labored and uneven, his body still pressed against hers.

Kate's reaction came swiftly as she stiffened and moved out of his embrace.

"Is it written somewhere that two old friends can't share a friendly kiss?" The words dropped like falling stones. But he heard even more in the brittle tone of her voice.

How could he be bitter, when he'd been the one to dare fate to take her from him? He remembered it all—everything he had given up—and he longed to fill his empty soul to overflowing....

FOR ONE CRAZY MOMENT Kate had felt alive while Cole gave her the kind of kiss she had only been able to dream about for the past year and a half. The next minute, he was dismissing the act as a mistake he wouldn't make again. She shook her head, regretting her own transparency. The one thing she didn't need was Cole back in her life, reminding her that the sexual chemistry they shared was potent enough to override her self-preservation. The kiss had left her with barely enough energy to follow him out of the car.

Though she sensed, rather than saw, the change in him, the effect it had on her was profound. Tears sprang into her eyes, and she had to blink them away. Damn him. Did he really think he could still take what he wanted and be on his way? Had she allowed that to happen again? She couldn't breathe. His presence still engulfed her. Worse, she found herself yearning for more. *He'll just throw you away again,* she chided herself.

Cole walked around to the passenger side of the car and placed his hands on the doorframe.

"You ready?" he asked in a husky, sensual voice.

"Just try and stop me," she replied, more seriously than not.

"Okay, then. You know what's coming next."

Kate filled her lungs with air to gather resolve. She was very much afraid she knew what was coming next.

The garage spilled over with cars, mostly media vans. There was plenty of time for their television-news crews to scoop a story. The night air had the biting effect of acupuncture, but it was exactly what Kate needed at the moment. She ran her tongue across her bruised lips, savoring the taste of Cole.

They had barely exited his unmarked car when a handful of reporters spotted Cole and began running toward him. Cole pulled her next to him with a strong arm. Flashbulbs flared and television cameras aimed their hooded lenses at Cole's stubborn features as he moved them through the sea of reporters with intention in his stride. He paused in the doorway of the hospital lobby, not from shyness, but for effect. One media person went into a cutaway. Questions flew like birds in a thunderstorm.

"I'll give you a statement as soon as I know something," Cole said, his voice firm, final.

"Any connection to the Hangman?" one reporter shouted.

"No comment," Cole replied in a monotone.

He picked up the pace again, and Kate was aware of him tightening his grip on her arm. Not once did she chance a glance in his direction. She was only aware that the swarm of reporters respected him, and stepped aside accordingly to make a path for them. He was a man of substance, and she felt a surge of admiration for him.

"What'd the victim see, Chief?" asked another. "Did you get a positive ID on the psycho?"

"Give me a chance to assess the situation," Cole said, gesturing with his hand, "then I'll brief you all at a press conference."

"Who's the woman with you? The victim's relative?"

"Can you give us a statement, lady? Were you at the crime scene when the shooting occurred?"

Cole tensed, then threw up his hand in disgust. The expression on his face alerted Kate to the fact that his restraint was wearing thin as the reporters fired questions at them.

"The lady is Federal Agent Quin," Cole snapped, silencing the inappropriately excited reporters as he guided Kate through the glass entrance to Our Lady of Grace Neurological Center. "Now how 'bout showing the feds that we know how to roll out the red carpet out here in the Southwest?"

"Give us something, Chief! How did he slip a weapon inside the courthouse? Is he a cop?"

As if they wanted him to be. They wanted a pound of flesh, Cole's flesh, and Kate could see the bite marks on him.

"If you hungry wolves will give me breathing room," he said in the controlled voice he reserved for nuisance reporters, "I'll check with the doctors first. Then I'll brief you." It satisfied them for the moment. Cole offered no explanations to Kate. "We'll take the service elevators," was all he whispered to her. He slipped a protective arm around her shoulder while he parted the throng of reporters with his other arm. Around the next corner they met a police guard positioned at the elevators, who okayed them to go to the fifth floor.

The doors opened on cue, and Cole guided her into the empty elevator. He was standing close enough for her to feel his body heaving with each breath he drew. She thought her own heart was going to drill a hole right through her rib cage. But once the elevator doors slammed shut, he released her.

She took several deep breaths before she trusted herself to speak. "Were you serious about a press conference?"

"Just a stall tactic—time is on our side where the press is concerned."

At the fifth floor, the elevator doors slipped apart. Kate led the way out as a shiver rippled through her body, a stark reminder of the discipline that would be required of her for the next few weeks.

"Hello, Chief," another police officer said.

Cole nodded in recognition.

A handful of officers and hospital personnel littered the halls of the intensive-care facility. Otherwise, the place looked sterile, felt dead. The only thing missing was the antiseptic smell, Kate thought as the two of them hurried toward the information desk.

Cole withdrew his badge from his breast pocket and slapped it down on the countertop for the nurse to see before he spoke. "I'm Chief McGuire. The patient is Jane Doe. She was admitted a short time ago with a bullet wound to the head."

"Yes..." The nurse thumbed through pages attached to a clipboard. "She had been out of surgery about an hour when—"

What? Kate wanted to scream when the nurse abruptly broke off to answer the telephone. She glanced at Cole and saw from the tight expression on his face that his patience was growing thin.

"I'm sorry," the nurse resumed in a dull tone. "She surprised everyone when she woke up."

"Where is she?" Cole asked, an edge of tension creeping into his voice.

"A very unfortunate thing happened...."

"What? What unfortunate thing?"

Kate cast a curious glance toward the two uniformed men flanking a doorway on the right side of the hallway a few feet down the corridor. If Jane Doe was dead, then why were the guards still hanging around?

"She's back in surgery." The nurse's mouth was working again. "She suffered a stroke... it's not uncommon to throw a clot—"

"What's her prognosis?" Kate intervened.

"Extremely critical."

"Damn!" Cole muttered, giving Kate a desperate look.

"Is there anything else?" the nurse asked.

This was intended as a dismissal, but Kate was more concerned with the victim than the woman in the white uniform.

"Yes," Kate said. "There is."

She had to ask questions; the drill was the most important part of her job—and an inherent part of *her.*

"There's nothing else I know to tell you." The nurse was moving around the counter to usher them out when the doctor arrived. He was tall and thin, in his late forties, and serious-faced. The smell of antiseptic preceded the man stepping toward them. It nauseated Kate.

"I'm Dr. List," he said, without extending his hand. He was rubbing his arms with something Kate suspected to be the source of the foul smell.

The introductions were brief. Kate read the evasion in the doctor's eyes and addressed it first. "Did she survive the surgery?"

"Her condition is critical," the doctor said in a monotone. "It will be some time before the anesthetic has entirely worn off, and we know if she'll be able to breathe on her own. Meanwhile, we have her hooked up to life supports."

"Is there brain activity?" she asked, while a hundred other questions lined up inside her head.

He nodded, but what he said next was not as favorable. "This kind of situation can go either way. The bullet lodged inside her head—possibly saving her life. Exit wounds do irreparable damage. Should the victim survive, the possibility of a future stroke will constantly cloud her life." He politely paused to allow them time to absorb that. "It's difficult to determine the extent of brain damage—her speech center will be impaired—and there could be permanent paralysis. But for the time being, it's another case of hurry up and wait."

Hurry up and wait. The words struck her ears like a clap of thunder. The doctor looked from one to the other for a polite ten seconds, then excused himself. But Kate wasn't through with him yet. Had the victim been examined for trace evidence? The drill continued.

"Please, Doctor," Kate said. "Just one more question."

The doctor sighed wearily and frowned his capitulation.

"How soon will you allow a pathologist to examine the body?"

"Miss—"

"Agent Quin," Kate said, flashing the smile she normally reserved for door-to-door solicitors.

Unimpressed, he nodded acknowledgment and started speaking. "Jane Doe arrived on a stretcher. Not in a body bag." He viewed her with the expression of a professional who'd just been asked to compromise his integrity.

Thank you, indeed, for that revelation, she thought.

"Is there any point?" Cole asked. "Superior court isn't your ideal closed environment."

"I want everything—hair and fiber workups, latent prints...."

"I wouldn't hold my breath," Cole murmured.

The frown between his brows reflected genuine frustration. She pressed her lips together, annoyed at his lack of support.

Sifting over a live victim for trace evidence had not been a consideration for Kate prior to Jane Doe. That was usually reserved for the offenders. But she had a job to do, too, whether Cole appreciated her efforts or not.

After a moment, she pressed on, confident about the importance of her request.

"Dr. List, I'd like permission for our forensic pathologist to use your lab to examine the victim." The words bumped into one another as she spewed them all in one breath.

"I don't know. That's highly unusual." He fixed his sunken eyes on hers. "The woman isn't dead yet."

She looked to Cole for support. His expression had become glazed, all emotion seeming to have drained from his face.

"That the body is still warm doesn't mitigate the trace evidence we might find there," Cole said, his voice taking on a hard edge. Another revelation.

"Victims have rights, too," the doctor protested strongly.

"Not with this madman on the loose," Cole had to remind him. "We owe it to this woman to try and find out who inflicted the injuries."

Kate looked up at Cole for a moment, assessing the resolution in his face, measuring the strength in his features. What he had just done spoke volumes. Admiration welled up inside her.

"All right." The doctor relented. "I'll make the arrangements. Check back at the nurses' station."

Kate glanced at Cole and released the breath she hadn't realized she'd been holding. She saw that he noticed—and that he couldn't stop himself from smiling a little.

"Thank you, Doctor," Kate managed to say, and she knew she sounded unnerved. She realized, too, there might not be any better chance to get this close to the psychopath. "We'll need elimination prints from everyone at the hospital who has handled the victim."

The doctor's obvious irritation with Kate moved her not one way or the other. The possibility of finding something the killer had left behind sent her thoughts spiraling.

There were a lot of things about her job that weren't wonderful. This victim could die. The inalterable statement made her sad as hell. And *that* made her strong.

"Did the victim say anything?" Cole asked.

The doctor had turned to leave. "Nothing I heard. But I was told she began talking just prior to the stroke," he admitted. "You'll have to ask your detective what she said. He didn't confide in me."

Kate did her best to look properly solemn, but this might just be the break they needed to get the investigation on track.

Chapter Four

"The world is a cruel place, ain't it, Chief?"

Inside the patient ICU room, a husky, broad-shouldered man was lounging on a chair. His stubby legs were extended to their full length and balanced on their heels. One hand cushioned his head against the wall, the other rested on a holstered gun.

"I figured I'd find you in here holding up the wall," Cole said.

Kate was certain the man was a cop, although in San Domingo anyone could carry a weapon. But his five o'clock shadow was certainly a tip-off to her that he didn't belong in front of a television camera.

"Throw me some good news, Scoot," Cole said. "We're sinking fast."

The man eased one ankle up over a knee and adjusted his sock. "I wouldn't hold my breath."

"Regale me," Cole persisted. "I'm all ears. Did the victim talk or not?"

"She talked," Scoot growled, showing his teeth by curling his upper lip like a dog with a bad disposition.

That's the way it was with some men, especially cops, Kate thought. They covered their affection with rudeness. If she was right, these two were close. Cole lifted his eyebrows and splayed his hands, palm side up, as if to say "Toss me the ball."

"She didn't say anything worth telling. It'll all be in my report," Scoot said, then cast a curious eye at Kate.

Kate gave him a long steady look, and summed him up as a garden-variety detective who hid his shortcomings behind an impenetrable facade.

"Just for the hell of it," Cole said, "tell me anyway."

Scoot spread his lips into a toothy smile. "Relative?" he asked, still scrutinizing Kate.

She met his stare, cool for cool. She wasn't impressed, but he had successfully deflected Cole's question until he could qualify her.

"No, and stand up, dammit," Cole barked. "Shake hands with Agent Quin."

Scoot heaved himself to his feet, while more grimace than grin stretched his face during the introduction. He was a bulky, lumbering man. "Hey-y-y, I ain't putting my palm against one belonging to some mind-reading Bureau agent."

Point-blank. Kate never saw it coming. He'd made it clear that he didn't think psychiatrists or psychologists had any business pretending to be experts in profiling criminal suspects. But she wasn't accusing him of depth, either.

"Kate, meet Scoot Grasso, my chief of detectives."

"I'm flattered, Detective," Kate purred, feeling the advancing warmth of self-satisfaction. "But you overrate my talent—although I'm certain there's plenty to be gleaned from *your* palm."

"Don't take him personally," Cole said. "He's rude to everybody, but he makes up for it with a wealth of good information."

At least he had stood, the act requiring the effort of a man years older than what Kate estimated the detective to be. The cop hooked his thumbs in his belt and hoisted up his slacks as he stared at her with unyielding eyes that he kept constantly narrowed—for surveillance, she eventually decided.

"Glad to meet you," Kate said, extending her arm and giving him the smile she reserved for the press and other irritants. Kate suffered no misgivings. Scoot would help her if he had to, if his chief ordered him to; otherwise, it was Intruder Beware.

"Likewise," Scoot grumbled, refusing her outstretched hand, which wilted like a thirsty flower.

"Chief tells me you're here to put some new wheels on the investigation."

Kate glanced over at Cole. He grinned and lifted his eyebrows.

"We got ourselves a clean freak," Scoot tossed out on the table for the two of them to devour. "The victim looked tidy as hell, considering the amount of lead in her head. Swelling didn't help, though," he added. "But I got a fix on her. The picture and description on her license was enough to ID her—just barely." Kate's heart jumped. "Phyllis Coffer—you know the one,

Chief—drew a hung jury in McGuire's court today. The judge cut her loose and she walked."

The detective gave them the news casually. But Kate glanced at Cole. From the expression on his face, she could tell that he'd been just as shocked as she by the revelation. The investigation moved another tick forward, and her stomach flip-flopped.

"What did you find in her purse?" Kate prodded. "Phone messages? Mail? Maybe—"

Scoot looked as though he might blow a vessel.

"You thinking I missed something?" he snarled.

"Just checking."

Scoot stiffened. "I don't believe this," he sputtered. "You feds have no shame."

"Simple task," Cole offered as evidence he intended to back Kate.

Scoot wiggled his eyebrows. "Yeah," he grumbled. "The CSU boys latched on to it." Scoot's face became a mask, his expression pleasant but impenetrable. "Even you feds know the drill. When they got something to say, they'll let you know."

Relief filled Kate that the crime-scene unit was handling the victim's purse and its contents as evidence. She wasn't ruling out latent prints.

Seconds later, Cole voiced a point that was already on her mind. "When our friend from city hall shows up—and he will—we don't know anything. This victim's a Jane Doe."

Kate allowed her thoughts to roam back over her conversation with the mayor, allowing all of it to sink in.

"What difference does it make?" Scoot asked. "This nutball's into fantasy, anyway. He's just warming up for the next one. He ain't coming back for her."

"Kate?" Cole prompted.

Kate kept her tone reasonable, though she realized the urgency. "Why not allow the press to count her as another statistic?"

"As in dead?" Scoot barked.

"The killer doesn't need the added aggravation of a failure," she said. "It might urge him out of his cooling-down period, have him on the attack again."

"You want a theory?" Scoot plowed on with the tenacity of an ox.

About as much as she wanted another victim. Everybody had a theory, she thought, looking to Cole. He exchanged a knowing glance with her, then rubbed his eyes, fighting back fatigue. It was apparent he'd been giving this investigation everything he had and then some. She felt an overwhelming urge to comfort him; propriety prevented her from doing so in front of the lumbering detective.

"I think our guy knew her."

Cole turned slightly to contemplate his C of D. "What?"

"I think he knew her. Either that or he was someone who had access."

"Makes sense," Kate said, easing into the conversation.

"I think we might have ourselves a little singing canary," Scoot bulldozed on.

He would take his time with the good information. Kate was certain that he had stashed a nugget to toss out for show. She realized he was having fun with it.

"It's a good thing you happened along," he told her in a tone that said that in the unlikely event they shared the pleasure of working together, their union would produce the odd couple. In the next breath he added, "Chief tells me you like keeping company with weirdos."

Although she was feeling impatient, Kate had the wit to reply, "The price for catching a psychopath," delivering the words with sufficient impact to further loosen Scoot's tongue.

"Wouldn't you know it," he said, looking from her to Cole. "The victim wakes up and starts moaning and jabbering."

The tips of Cole's ears turned bright red.

"Cough it up before I strangle it out of you," Cole grumbled.

"'Please...help me,' she's pleading, you know? Like she's desperate or something."

Phyllis Coffer did not want to die. The magnitude of her fright sickened Kate. It was difficult for her to listen to Scoot mimicking the victim.

"Kind of like she's going in and out of her head." The notion rendered a belly laugh from the depths of his ample girth. "A regular out-of-body experience." The smile faded. "She keeps this up until the lights go out." He paused for effect, because he knew he had hooked them.

"The lights?" Kate questioned, expecting Scoot to supply logic.

He knew how to shock, too.

"Yeah," he said. "She blows a blood clot."

"Is that it?" Cole asked.

"You know me, Chief. I've got a long memory. If there was another verse to the song, I'd sing it to you."

"Were there any apparent defense wounds to indicate the victim might have fought back?" Kate asked.

"No," Scoot said flatly.

"Did you check for broken fingernails—her hands and arms for scratch marks?"

Scoot lit a cigarette and sucked hard on it until the tip was blazing. Kate considered reminding him of the No Smoking rules, but thought better of it as the detective looked over at her and flicked an ash.

"I know what defense injuries are," he assured her while smoke spewed from both nostrils. "Hell, she probably didn't know what hit her. It's clear to me that the perp had the element of surprise on his side. You agree, Doc?"

"How many shots were fired?" Kate asked, deflecting his question as calmly as possible.

"We've got a .38 slug inside the victim's head," Scoot said. "She was running when he plugged her—heading for the ladies' bathroom. This one he nailed from behind."

Kate thought about those last few seconds the victim had to think about her fate. What kind of monster could impose that degree of fear? The questions were stacking up too fast inside her head. Without ballistics on the bullet, they needed trace evidence, and Kate made a mental note to have Forensics wave the laser wand over the victim, also.

Cole's beeper sounded. One of them, at least, had been spared.

"You two should have plenty to talk about," Cole said. "I won't be gone long." He was looking at Scoot who was grunting his displeasure, refusing to give an inch. Cole's brows lifted as Scoot hesitated.

"Well... I'm on duty," the detective argued.

"You're *always* on duty." Cole lifted his chin in Kate's direction. "Bring Agent Quin on-line with the investigation."

"Yeah," his C of D capitulated, wearing the face of the happy hunter who'd just been denied the bag of a lifetime. "I guess I can do that."

"I think you'd better," Cole advised. To Kate, he added, "You're in good hands."

"Oh?" she queried, glancing at Scoot's beefy paws.

All that needed to be said was there in Cole's eyes, but had he been reading hers, he would have known that she wasn't about to be *handled.* Not by the likes of Scoot.

WORKING WITH KATE on this case was possibly the most important role Cole had ever played in his life. And he had only one chance to get it right.

In the five or so minutes he'd been gone to make his phone call, Kate and his C of D had pulled off a remarkable disappearing act. A surge of exasperation was threatening to shatter his control when he spotted her—minus Scoot. His current state of exhaustion notwithstanding, he decided they both needed a coffee break.

"Where's Scoot?"

Kate shrugged. "Disappeared. I decided to look for you instead."

"Hmm. How 'bout I buy you a cup of coffee for making the right choice?"

Kate made a face, implying refreshment was long overdue.

The hospital cafeteria would have to suffice. Cole led the way. It would also have to be quick, because he had a hidden agenda.

"Patio okay?" he asked as they strode into the dimly lit room.

At this time of night, the hospital cafeteria was lifeless. The only sounds, other than their own, were coming from the intercom. The aroma of hot coffee filled him at once, easing his guilt for the delay, even though he realized the crime scene was icing up with every passing minute.

"Patio's fine," she said.

Cole was looking for the right opportunity to send up the flare while he set about getting their coffee and doughnuts.

"I'll find a table outside," she said levelly.

He followed her into the brisk night air, cool enough by now that he could see his breath. He was grateful for his leather jacket.

"You cold?" he asked.

"My layered clothing is finally serving its purpose."

Kate seated herself at the closest table, and Cole arrived with a tray loaded with coffee and jelly doughnuts. Some things, he remembered.

"Have one." He pointed at the tray.

"Thanks." She took a generous bite.

"We have to talk," he announced in his no-nonsense voice. "Lay our cards on the table. Be up-front with each other."

"Up-front?" she whispered, once she had swallowed the mouthful of doughnut. "What do you mean, 'up-front'?"

"I mean open—with the investigation," Cole clarified, as if she should have known. "Damn, it's cold out here. Want to move inside?"

Her mouth was full again, so she just shook her head.

"I can be stubborn, Kate," he said in a tone filled with mounting excitement. "But I have to know where you stand."

Kate watched and listened to him run the gamut of his emotions. Her eyes beseeched him. "All this because of the mayor?"

"Are you with me? I don't mean to put pressure on you, I just want to know—I *need* to know that now."

"What the mayor wants—"

"I don't care about what he wants," he insisted. "This investigation is my responsibility. I call the shots. It's all on my head. In or out, Kate?"

She had to take a sip of coffee. Several sips.

"That's easy," she said softly. "The lack of choices makes it easy."

She arched her eyebrows and nodded. He swallowed the acknowledgement and heaved a great sigh, then smiled his approval.

"Thanks." His voice faltered. He rolled his shoulders to work out some of the tension, rubbed his face with the open palms of his hands. Pushing his weariness aside with an effort, he smiled. "*We'll* be able to live with the results."

Kate choked that nugget of information down with too-strong black coffee. She took a long look at Cole, as though trying to read his face. For a brief moment he let himself think about how it would feel to make love to her again.

"Nothing's more important than getting a handle on this investigation," she said.

Cole nodded and sipped his coffee, while he puzzled something.

"What is it?" she asked, her attention fully captured.

"I need your word on something, Kate."

"I just gave it to you," she said. "There's more?"

"Everything gets cleared through my office. Is that a problem for you?"

Kate was clearly torn. She sipped her coffee in an attempt to buy time. All the while her eyelids remained hooded, hiding her internal conflict.

She took a deep breath, then said, "It goes with the territory. Anyway, you know me better. I don't leapfrog."

"I know. But I needed to hear it from you."

"I'm on your side, but I don't think you're hearing what I'm trying to tell you."

"What's that?"

"Nothing's more important than the investigation. Politics, personalities, differences—none of that matters here, Cole. We have a job to do."

At the moment, nothing was more important to Cole than having Kate back. Didn't he, at the very least, owe her that truth?

Chapter Five

"Where is the forensic pathologist?" Kate asked the uniformed men flanking the fourth-floor superior-court elevator doors, open wide and barred by a yellow ribbon of tape, warning: Crime Scene—Do Not Cross.

The ornate wall clock registered ten-thirty. She thought the most obvious evidence of crime was the persistent smell of disinfectant in the air. Officers loitered everywhere, and except for the security guard, everyone was friendly, backslapping, taking pictures.

"Picked up his bag and left 'bout an hour ago," one of the officers said, lifting the bright yellow ribbon. "Said he was on his way to the hospital."

The odor of cleanser nearly gagged Kate. Was the pungent scent floating up from the floor a telltale sign of a hodgepodge cleanup effort? The wave of panic passed as she noted the floor and walls, decorated in obvious blood splatters in shapes and colors suitable for tie-dying.

"Watch where you step," Cole cautioned, sounding protective without being condescending.

The interior walls of the superior-court building were painted white, but had turned a yellowish brown, much like old shellac. The foyer was in the exact center of the building and extended from the lobby all the way to the top floor. It would have been easy to search the building, Kate thought, puzzled at the possibility of the killer carrying a weapon and making his way inside the confines of this legal bastion. It occurred to her that he would encounter the same difficulties in attempting to smuggle his weapon out of the building.

It was turning eerily quiet. The crime-scene people had already moved in and moved out, carrying their kit bags, cameras, and vacuum cleaners. The physical evidence had been recovered. Kate hoped it would be enough.

"You okay?" came Cole's attentive voice.

She turned to face him, but something else had caught his eye.

"That looks like blood," he muttered to himself.

"It is," Kate said, while a mental image flashed through her mind of Phyllis Coffer running for her life.

The flat feeling descended again. Kate was tasting the sickening fear when a tiny thought particle wiggled loose from her paralyzed brain. The blood spatters on the wall closest to Judge McGuire's chamber doors told Kate that Phyllis Coffer had been shot in the foyer. The absence of drag marks suggested that the killer had then carried the victim into the lavatory on the other side of the room.

"Do you have a general idea of the victim's body size?" Kate asked.

"Around five foot six or seven inches, fleshy. One hundred and twenty, maybe more."

Kate considered that a moment. "He carried her to the bathroom, because the stalls gave him a convenient place to hang her."

"So you think he was large, strong?"

"Maybe. But we can't rule out adrenaline compensating for his size."

"And he also wanted to tidy up her body."

It was not unheard of for a killer to feel remorse after his sadistic act. But the glaring contradiction of this post-offense behavior with each of the victims puzzled her.

At first, no one noticed the elevator doors splitting apart, until a voice sprang from the steel enclosure.

"Mother-of-pearl!" exclaimed the thick woman who was herself pressed into a steel box of sorts, one with wheels. Her muscular arms efficiently propelled her wheelchair toward them. The elevator doors swished shut behind her, sending wafts of "Paris" perfume into the air ahead.

"Who let you in, Grace?" Cole asked her.

"Is that any way to greet an old friend?"

Leathery skin, from too much sun, had probably aged her beyond her years, Kate decided. Reddish-brown hair, long and curly, was neatly pulled into a fifties-style ponytail complete with a pompadour bang.

"I'm waiting," he said.

"You know I'm a nocturnal creature."

"Visiting at all hours of the night is bad manners."

"Fact is, I've been here all day. Never left. I covered the angel-of-mercy case in Judge McGuire's court. The jury returned a verdict at four o'clock, and I was hustling interviews until five when I had an appointment with your dad."

"Did you meet with him?" Kate asked.

Grace paused, challenging Kate to a visual duel. Kate gauged her to be about forty-five. Aging bluish green eyes had probably once been the focal point of her face, but her wary stare showed signs of burnout. Kate wondered about her career. The woman probably needed a vacation, but this story was hot enough to pay a hungry reporter's back rent in any district. Kate could understand Grace's tenacity.

"No. But I did see Simon LaRoush and Nan Dupree."

Seized with curiosity, Kate prodded Grace to elaborate. "That's not unusual. They both work here."

"True enough," Grace allowed in a tone that said she was saving the punch for the last. "But every time I see them, they're fighting."

Grace was toying with her. Kate waited.

"Not today, though. Nan's crying and taking on while Simon's trying to comfort her. I was a bit disappointed in them. I do so love to watch Nan tear into

LaRoush after he's taken apart the defense attorney's case."

"Grace," Cole chided, "you don't have a reverent bone in your body."

His voice sounded low and husky, and he flashed Grace that half grin with those wonderful lips. To distract herself, Kate made a mental note to follow up on the details of the angel-of-mercy case from the court's docket.

"See anybody else?" Cole asked.

"Besides the guard? No." Grace lowered her tone to a whisper. "Rumor has it Phyllis Coffer is the victim."

Kate had always admired Cole's calm, his ability to dangle the bait. It startled her to see him so taken aback by the reporter's remark.

"I wouldn't jump to any conclusions if I were you," Cole said, his expression implying that anything he said on the subject was still clouded with doubt.

"Never mind about the dead," Grace insisted.

"Who said anything about anyone being dead?"

There was confusion in Grace's expression when she prompted, "She's *alive?*"

It was an old journalism trick, but Kate had no way of knowing whether Cole had been taken by the reporter, or whether he'd intended to throw her that bone.

"If she's alive," Grace boasted, "she won't be for long. The human body wasn't designed to accommodate a .38 slug." She paused. "You playing this one close to the chest, Chief?"

"Nope," Cole said flatly. "I just don't know anything yet. You may have to figure it out for yourself."

"I believe I have, and it's not good. But if our angel of mercy talks, seat me ringside." She had turned her intense gaze on Kate. "Now then, who is this living beauty with you? No, wait! *What* is she doing with you? I think you've outdone yourself."

"She's more than capable of handling herself," Cole returned, his eyes on Kate.

Kate only wished that were true.

"She's a fed," he went on, "so watch your mouth." Cole turned to look at Kate again. "Kate, meet investigative reporter Grace Van Buren. You'll want to watch what you say, too."

She liked Grace at once. Confident, intelligent, wry of speech and keen of eye, she was not one of those fast-talking reporters whose questions were meant to satisfy the brain-dead readers of tabloids.

"I've read your work," Kate said.

She had also read about the journalist losing her legs in a car bombing. The investigative reporter got too close to organized crime. The syndicate got even. Or so speculation went. To date, no one had atoned for the deed—except Grace, who had paid with her legs and had almost lost her career.

Grace launched the conversation with, "Well, Kate, isn't it exciting? Don't you agree it's going to be impossible to keep our eyes focused on all the routine, boring local news when this fascinating maniac is in town?"

"I don't know," Kate said, far too clever to respond to cleverly disguised declarative statements made by a member of the press. "What do you think?"

"How'd you latch on to her?" Grace asked Cole. "She's a sharp one."

"Sharp enough," Cole agreed. "Mention feds to Grace, and you see Pulitzer Prize written all over her. Right, Gracie?"

"I expect even we reporters sometimes have to do some thinking," Grace replied.

"That should take care of the need for an accurate dissemination of information to the public," Cole said, matching wits admirably, Kate thought.

"No reporter worth his paycheck is going to write a boring story," Grace informed them both.

"The problem here is interpretation of 'public interest,'" Cole said.

"Our relationship is far from blissful, but don't leave the poor girl thinking we're adversaries," Grace went on. "You see, Kate, we both understand each other and abide by certain principles of ethics and common courtesy."

"Sounds like a healthy relationship to me," Kate put in.

"I like this girl, Cole," Grace said. "She can help you if you'll allow it. This is a frightened city, Kate—frightened of you."

"Why me?"

"You're here to validate our worst fears. We already suspect a psychopath is on the loose. Cruelty is always shocking, don't you agree? I understand he socks an eye out of his victim by exploding a .38 slug into it—just before he hangs the corpse."

Grace paused for a moment, to gauge Kate's response. But Kate was far too disciplined to react.

"Tell us, Kate," Grace asked, "is this one living in the real world?"

"This is about as real as it gets."

Grace sighed. Then Cole's beeper sounded.

"You can't trust her, Kate," Cole cautioned with humor in his tone.

"There's nothing you might tell me about this case that I'll repeat to another living soul—unless I have your permission, my dear."

Kate smiled sweetly and watched as Cole strode out of the foyer and ducked into an office to use the telephone there.

"I'm not interested in attribution," Kate said, turning back to Grace.

The reporter didn't respond directly. But the expression on her face spoke her thoughts.

"Tell me, Kate, what's it like being a mind hunter? Getting inside a deranged soul? You and I are a great deal alike, you know."

Kate paused, knowing she was stepping onto the hard-packed turf of the media. "How so, Grace?"

"It's the thrill of going with our instincts.... That's what we thrive on. I find instinct infinitely more exciting than procedure," Grace murmured. She hesitated, then decided to push buttons. "What about you, Kate?"

Grace Van Buren smiled, but it failed to reach her troubled eyes. *A closet alcoholic? Certainly not drugs.*

"I never argue with basic police work. But when instinct is all you've got to go on," Kate said, annoyed at having her skills minimized by a reporter, "it's considered an advantage."

"I'm not without moral responsibility," Grace said, reaching for her cigarettes and finding the pack empty. "About the serial killings, if there's anything I can print to help you—"

Kate was more curious than annoyed by Grace's sophomoric approach to picking her brain. "The police have yet to determine whether we're dealing with a serial killer," she said.

"Then what are you doing here?"

"Looking for any obvious trace evidence."

"What's all this about evidence?" came Cole's deep voice.

"I like her," Grace said abruptly.

Cole passed his hand over his eyes. "I'm glad you approve."

Cole swung a loving arm around Grace, and Kate wondered about the extent of their relationship.

"Let's go get a drink," Grace suggested.

"You know the rules."

Grace only smiled. She clucked her tongue, then patted his arm. "Why, Chief, you know ethical responsibility never allows me to break the rules."

Cole wasted no time launching right into a set of questions for the reporter. "Speaking of ethics, how *did* you access the crime scene? And don't tell me you were in court today, because this happened after hours."

"You know what journalists are. Always nosing around. They're uncanny vermin."

"They're a darned nuisance," Cole countered.

"They have their uses, too," Kate joined in. "Love them or loathe them, but don't try to live without them."

"I'll show you to the elevator, Grace," Cole said.

"Damned if you will. I'll show myself out." The reporter impressively wheeled herself toward the silver cubicle. With practiced ease, she turned the chair around to enter backward. "I think it would be quite nice to know you, Kate. It would be a pity to have your trip cut short."

Kate listened with growing confusion, far too fatigued to puzzle out the point of Grace's ambiguous remark. The metal doors squeezed shut, and for the moment the cryptic meaning no longer mattered.

"She's the epitome of the curious reporter." Cole's voice was a welcome distraction. "Hey," he added, his tone low and beguiling, "you're tired."

To deny it would have been to lie, and she did neither. He would know otherwise.

"There's nothing else for us to accomplish tonight," she told him. "I'd rather have some preliminary lab results to sink my teeth into. And a list of everyone who was on or near the fourth floor of superior court this afternoon. Once I can sit down with them, I can begin to get a picture of what went on here this afternoon."

"We'll want to look into any threats. If our victim is anything, she's controversial. Scoot's filing an affidavit for a search warrant." He thought for a moment. "He should be able to hook a signature for the warrant from one of the commissioners in the initial-appearance court by morning. By then, we should have something back from the lab."

"I'm afraid the pickings are slim here. You were correct earlier. Superior court is not your ideal controlled environment." Kate pressed her lips together, but a sigh escaped her anyway.

"You've had a big day," Cole said, eyeing her.

Her stare conveyed what she was thinking.

"What a minute," he objected. "I'll admit that sounded—"

"Condescending?"

"Hungry?" he redirected. "I could take you back to my place, ply you with a home-cooked meal."

"You'd do the cooking?"

"I'm the only one who knows how."

Kate laughed, because the simple truth amused her. She shook her head. "I'm too tired." That, too, was the truth.

"Another time?"

She stared at him for a long moment, groping for the courage to say yes. When she didn't find it, she gave him the next best thing.

"Maybe," she said softly, and meant it.

IT WAS A START.

The ride to Wickenburg was quiet. Conversation

wasn't necessary. Neither needed small talk. It would have been excruciating when all he could think of was holding her and making love until the morning light.

Both were saturated with the details of the recent murder attempt. But his thoughts were far from the investigation that had been plaguing him for weeks. Cole wondered if Kate would invite him in. *It's too soon. Too many obstacles to be removed. Plenty of time...*

He pulled off the main road and eased down the driveway toward the guest cottage. Stopping in front of it, he turned off the engine. "I'll walk you to the door," he offered.

Was it disappointment he saw in her face? Did she dread the night to end, too?

She slid out of the passenger side before he could get around to open her door.

As they walked, he found himself tensing up like a teenager on his first date. This was ridiculous. He was thirty-four years old.

A few short steps and they were on the porch. The night breeze was chilly, and Cole dug his hands deeper into the pockets of his leather jacket. "I'll pick you up in the morning around seven o'clock," he said.

"I'll have coffee ready."

He curled his hands into fists before he could give in to the urge to touch her. "You might want to go for a swim," he suggested, his limbs aching at the thought of Kate's body in—and out—of a bathing suit.

Kate shivered. "Does Libby keep the water heated?"

He nodded. He thought, but couldn't be certain in the dimness of the porch, that her eyes were glowing above the gentle smile that suddenly appeared on her face. He lifted a finger to caress her cheek, and felt heat there.

He saw her open her mouth to speak, but drop her head instead. The act sent fire coursing through his veins. He wanted to mold her body against his where it belonged, to wrap his arms around her.... *Go. Before you beg.*

"Good night, Kate," he murmured, then turned his back on her before the look in her eyes could zap what was left of his willpower.

"Cole?"

He felt the tender pressure of her hand on his shoulder, freezing him in his tracks with power equal to an electrical current. He swung around to face her with the enthusiasm of a child who'd just been exonerated of some terrible wrongdoing.

"Thanks for thinking of it," she whispered.

He swallowed. The bathing suit flashed before his eyes again, and he struggled to dispel the image.

"Got any jeans to wear with those tennis shoes?" he asked huskily.

"They're the staple of my wardrobe."

"It might be a good idea to wear them tomorrow."

Reluctantly, he stepped away. Right now, as much as he longed to hold her, all he could embrace was hope—hope that she would soon allow him into her life again.

As determined as he was to win her back, he was also determined not to give in to the temptation of crossing over her personal and private threshold. Not yet. Not until he could prove to her that she could trust him.

Chapter Six

Kate was waiting for Cole when he arrived precisely at seven o'clock that morning. Her dreams had turned on her like a demon during the night. Over and over again she'd replayed the scene when he'd told her they should see other people. Like a fist, the words had slammed against her heart, where the emotional ties had remained securely in place despite an eighteen-month absence.

"Coffee?" she asked, the moment he was inside.

"Thanks, no. We'd better get going."

"What's up?"

"Nothing new. I thought we might devote the morning to setting you up at headquarters."

"I'll get my briefcase."

She wasted no time getting to the car. Under the circumstances, she considered Cole's offer to install her in a temporary office to be generous. She accepted it as a silent truce, and was grateful for it. It was an effort to control her seesawing emotions during the fifteen-mile ride to the San Domingo police headquarters.

Cole parked the Caprice in his reserved space and emerged from the car in silence. They entered the building by the rear door, and Kate wondered briefly if he was trying to slip her in without notice. Quickly, though, she changed her mind. She was being too defensive. As she followed Cole into the boxy, single-story adobe structure, she felt relief at his change of heart toward her position here. She'd been too hard on Cole. He deserved a chance.

The squad room was crammed to capacity with antiquated wooden desks. The paraphernalia of investigative police work filled the area to overflowing. There were a dozen or so telephones cluttering the scarred desktops, their bells at times sounding in unison. Uniformed cops and off-duty detectives congregated inside the inadequate task-force room, sipping coffee and exchanging information.

Kate felt growing uncertainty about Cole's ability to provide her with space. She followed him inside his glass-walled office. He threw his coat over a chair and rolled up his sleeves.

"Let's get started, shall we?" he said.

She nodded approval, wondering how he intended to pull off this magic act. He led her back out into one corner of the squad room. He patted a battered desk, saying, "This one's yours."

Terrific. "Thanks," she managed to mumble.

To isolate her from the rest of the room, he dragged over several freestanding partitions to section off the corner. Then he dragged in a couple of chairs, a file cabinet, chalkboard, typewriter, and a computer terminal.

"Sorry I don't have a secretary to offer."

"What you've put together is more than enough," she said, and meant it. "I'll need a few minutes to put my house in order."

"Take all the time you need. I'll see you at ten o'clock. I've called a task-force meeting. I'd like you to brief the men."

"Thanks, Cole."

"What for? I'm just doing my job," he said, backing away.

He bumped heavily into one of the partitions. His face flushed as she helped brace him upright. As automatic as her response had been, she had the sudden feeling that he was hot, molten lava and she risked getting burned. She removed her hands quickly.

"Cole, do you have any pull over at superior court?"

"Not an ounce, and I wouldn't advise you to use my name if you call, but . . . there's a gal over there in Records named Cora. . . ."

"Thanks. And I'll need a runner."

"Use Sal. He's backup on the radio, spends most of his day holding down a chair."

"Okay. See you."

"See you," he echoed, this time watching where he was going.

Kate wet her suddenly dry lips. A wave of peace washed over her, because she'd dared to drop her professional guard a notch with him, to ask him for help. It made a mockery of all she hid from him personally. She would deal with that later, she prayed, when she found some concrete answers, some peace, some resolve. But not now.

"I'M GLAD TO SEE SHE ain't bunking with the mayor," Scoot grumbled.

"There's room for two agencies here," Cole said.

Scoot wasn't quite convinced of that.

"As long as we're working parallel," the detective said. "The men ain't gonna take kindly to sharing their space with a fed. They need to know who's in charge."

"If they don't know, it won't do any good for me to tell them." Cole glanced over at the remains in the coffeepot on the hot plate, then changed his mind about having some.

"A sharp woman like her keeps you on your toes. Always making you think, else she gets ahead of you. Know what I mean?"

Cole scowled at Scoot and turned abruptly to collect Kate. He came up beside her, leaning close to her ear.

"Has anyone ever told you how sexy you look in jeans and a baggy sweatshirt?" he whispered.

Her expression changed subtly. "Privileged information, Chief."

He grinned at her, momentarily lighthearted. "Thanks for being a good sport about the makeshift quarters."

"Goes with the territory," she said softly.

He moved to the front then, motioning for Kate to take the seat beside him at the head of the cramped table. Once there, he looked across the room.

The troops were exhausted from pulling back-to-back shifts, from manning the telephones on their days off, from chasing down leads while on overtime. And now he had to introduce them to the federal agent who was here to tell them how to do their jobs.

But he was faced with an even greater dilemma: How was he going to deal with the conflict between his feelings for Kate and his sense of how the investigation should proceed? If he wasn't careful, he could lose his head. Tension was back full force, tightening his neck muscles while a vein throbbed in his temple. He sucked in a deep breath, hoping it would galvanize him into action. The buzz died down.

The investigation is all that matters. He would forget her and just do his job the best way he could. His department made a difference, and if she couldn't see that, then to hell with her!

"If I may quote the mayor," Cole began, "'This investigation needs a magic act.'" The declaration brought no comfort. "He's got Agent Quin hard at work on hooking up a hot line straight into this psycho's head."

"Any of you want to talk to the killer," Scoot put in, pulling a cloud of smoke deep into his lungs, "get with Agent Quin."

"Dial M for mind reader," a plainclothes detective clowned.

Kate's stricken face flamed with color. Accusations were rampant in her eyes as she glared at Cole. *How could you?* they demanded.

"Damn you," she whispered. "I dropped my guard, and you used it against me first chance you had."

"Kate, this has nothing to do with—"

"Thank you, Chief," she said too sweetly as she stood. A dramatic pause followed while she looked about the room. "If you were expecting Houdini, you're going to be disappointed. I have no rabbit to pull out of a hat. But if I did," she continued in clipped tones, "I would expect you to examine it."

She'd cut them down to size with one clean slice.

"I'll bet she even profiles her dates before she goes out," a veteran officer mused from the back of the room.

"I don't discuss my private life," Kate said, "except to say I carry a very fat briefcase home every night."

"What kind of nutball do we have on our hands?" Scoot asked, posing the first serious question. "He cleans up corpses."

Kate lifted a brow. "I'd use the word *tidy.*"

"A *clean freak*?" he echoed

"Labels tend to generalize," she cautioned. "I can't give you a thorough profile without additional study, but if it's a general term you're looking for, psychopath will do."

"Tell us something we don't already know," a uniformed officer said, sounding off from the front row. "Who ain't crazy?"

The rest of the group agreed. The rumblings among the men intensified.

"*Crazy,* as you put it," Kate began, "is a legal expression. But I suspect, before this is over with, *insanity* will become an issue.

"What's it gonna gain us to play mind games?" another uniform demanded.

The full strength of the afternoon sun was on her face. She appeared flushed as she spoke. "My work is not about *mind games,*" she said. "And I'm not talking about clairvoyant powers." She stared at Cole. The room turned eerily quiet. "I've been schooled to draw detailed portraits of killers by focusing on how they commit their crimes." The words came out without expression. Her eyes remained fixed on his. "That ability comes from experience. I've seen the worst of the worst." She paused to allow for challenging remarks. When there were none, she continued, "Considering the situation in San Domingo—3.5 bodies, and no one to pin responsibility on—I'd say your team could use another player, Chief McGuire. I want to emphasize to you that I am a team player."

"Thank you, Agent Quin," Cole said, finally.

"You've nothing to thank me for at this point," she responded flatly, refusing now to meet his gaze as he took the floor.

She seemed to be trying to pull her emotions together before they flew out of control. She'd been openly ridiculed—though she'd handled herself well—and he was responsible.

Somehow Cole stumbled through the presentation of the lab reports. When he finished, Kate was alredy working her way to the door. He lost sight of her as the policemen swarmed out of the room.

"Kate?" he called when he finally spotted her. "Wait a minute."

She didn't answer. Instead, she pushed toward the exit, heading outside.

Cole flew after her, squeezing past the others and darting through doors to catch up with her.

"I know what you're thinking," he began.

"Oh, please, don't make it worse. I don't have time for your macho games. While you were in there flexing your muscle for your men, this city was dealing with a highly stressed psychopath."

"I want him caught and locked away just as badly as you do," Cole said.

"You have an odd way of demonstrating it."

The back door continued to open and close, and the parking lot filled with the noise of departing cars and the smell of gas fumes.

"Blame it on whatever you like," she said, "but that won't change anything." Her eyes glistened, and her face seemed to lose all color. "You deliberately set me up in front of your men—turned them loose on me—did nothing to defend me."

"They're stressed tight, Kate. Don't take their behavior personally. They were just unwinding."

"At my expense," she snapped.

"Come on back inside with me. Let's talk."

"No."

It hurt—her resistance, her rejection of the comfort he needed to give. It hurt enough that he drew away. She wheeled around and headed back inside alone. He stood watching, frozen to the spot, his heart sinking like an anchor. It was several minutes before he decided to go inside, too. But first he had to get past Scoot, observing from the steps leading to the back door while he stuffed something in his face.

"You just gonna let her go?" Scoot asked. The detective shoved the last of a jelly doughnut into his mouth, chewed hurriedly, and swallowed.

"Your latent nobility is tedious," Cole snapped.

"I'd go after her if I were you." Now his C of D stood with his hands in his pockets, pinning the fronts of his jacket behind his thick hips. "I ain't no mind reader, but I think she's upset."

"You think—"

Cole broke off abruptly, choked by frustration. They made a unique combination, he and his chief detective, but over the past year they'd become close personal friends. At times, Cole would swear they *could* read each other's minds.

"You're not still interested in her, are you?"

A yearning flared inside Cole, stirring the embers of a fire that had never burned itself out. But allowing his feelings to show would expose him clean to the bone. He could only be thankful he had so much on his mind. Between keeping the mayor from going for his throat, and trying to jump-start a stagnant investigation, he didn't have time to dwell on Kate.

"Don't be ridiculous," Cole answered. "She's a necessary nuisance."

"I hate it when you lie to me," his C of D said dryly.

HUMILIATION FLOODED through Kate. She wanted only solitude, and time to rebuild her defenses. Her mistake was in thinking that she could work with him. How could you work with someone you couldn't trust? Whatever progress she'd made in soothing her ego and alleviating the tension since stepping back into his life, had been blown to smithereens. Her wound was eighteen months old, but her pain was as sharp as a recent knife cut.

A healthy dose of hard work was the medicine she needed. She would spend the day perusing the case files and trying to flesh out a psychopathic killer. The combination would take anyone's mind off their problems. She sank into the ragged chair at the well-used desk in her makeshift office. Cole had set her up. Worse, she had *allowed* him to. Her mind became a logjam of thoughts, and she decided to pour herself into the police reports stacked high on her desk.

On the very top of the heap, she noticed an envelope with a note attached to it from Sal. Curiosity swamped her like a freak desert rainstorm as she withdrew the court dockets from the envelope. Then pressing herself into the surprising comfort of the battered chair and propping her legs on the desk, she began reading.

By three o'clock that afternoon Kate was nearly wrung dry. For the better part of four hours she'd immersed herself in the court files. The words squirmed in front of her like squirming, black snakes. Then a familiar sentence coiled and flung itself at her.

Kate held herself still as potentially venomous fangs struck at the base of her spine and a shooting spasm traveled the length of it. Sweat beaded on her forehead as she absorbed the revelation jumping out at her from the information contained within the court dockets.

Dimly, Kate could hear the steady hum of activity—phones, footsteps, voices—around her. But she was drifting away. When she found herself staring blindly into the room, she forced herself to re-examine the pages. Her heart hammered in her throat. She needed a drink, and the shock of cold water to her face. She couldn't swallow. Slowly, Kate eased out of the chair.

She found the bathroom down the hall. Inside, she splashed herself with water, then glimpsed her face in the mirror as she patted herself dry with a paper towel. Her cheeks were white, her eyes enormous. She was aware of many things. But foremost, that she'd possibly found the common denominator in the case.

Find Cole, the voice of conscience told her when she headed back to her office. She had just seated herself when Scoot lumbered in with a guest. The mayor was executing the same routine he had when she had first met him: adjusting a perfectly knotted tie, inspecting his jacket for lint, then adjusting the tie again.

"Agent Quin," Scoot announced from the edge of her desk, as though he were still a city block away, "the mayor here wants to talk to you."

And you're handling my appointments? she almost retorted.

Uninvited, the mayor seated himself with his usual bad manners. Scoot propped himself against a wall and stood there as though the wall depended on him to hold it up.

"Run down to the coffee machine and bring back some coffee, Detective," the mayor said condescendingly.

Scoot briefly considered this.

"Get yourself a cup, too."

Scoot was still thinking. "I could use a smoke," he mumbled.

"Go, then."

He did. But first he looked to Kate. She was trained to handle confrontations with men much more dangerous than elected officials, but Scoot was like a bulldog with an old shoe. He had a hard time letting go. She raised her eyebrows and sent Scoot a faint smile. Until she did, he dug in and stood his ground.

"We've got ourselves a crisis," the mayor pompously declared, once Scoot was gone.

We? Her face remained as rigid as plaster of paris. "That's why I'm here," she reminded him. "I've discovered something important." She felt a momentary attack of conscience, but after remembering Cole's lack of support during the briefing, she realized she was in this alone. She took a deep breath and pressed on. After all, she'd been brought into the case by the mayor, and her responsibility was to report to him.

"I'm glad you're here," she said finally. "I need to talk to you in the strictest confidence."

Mayor Madden was tentatively searching her face. "Enthrall me, Agent Quin," he said theatrically.

"I think I've found the common denominator for all the victims—"

"*What?*" he interrupted, and her uneasiness grew.

She swallowed and hoped the feelings he'd stirred weren't apparent in her voice.

"Was it reported to you that the victims each had legal histories?"

"No such thing was reported to me. Get to the point, Quin."

"Today I learned that their court adjudications coincided."

The revelation was followed by a dramatic pause while the mayor allowed her disclosure to hang on the stale air.

"Well, well, very good," he said grudgingly. "But how does this point us to the killer?"

"Judge McGuire exonerated each—"

"*McGuire?* What about him?"

His tone prompted Kate to respond, but instinct told her not to.

"The chief has been indisposed for comment about this detail," he continued. "I suspected as much from him."

"Well, obviously I missed something," she said shortly.

"McGuire has been withholding information critical to this investigation."

Scoot was quick to intervene. Kate had scarcely been aware of when he'd re-entered. He passed out coffee with a cigarette hanging from his mouth. He wouldn't look at the mayor. Or Kate.

The mayor was oblivious to Scoot's presence. "Of course, you realize it's in your best interests to assist me in handling the chief."

Handling? As in assailing? That got her full attention. At some point soon, Kate intended to take her cue to leave.

"I hope to interface with both you and the chief," she said.

For some inexplicable reason, the mayor was about to take Cole apart. Kate could hear her heartbeat. Her intention had not been to bash the chief of police.

"I think the chief should be here," Cole's C of D grumbled.

"I'm not interested in what you think," the mayor said coldly.

"It ain't what you're interested in that I was talkin' about," Scoot snarled. "It's days like today that make me wonder why I don't just put in my papers early."

He talked with his back to the mayor—there were so many ways to show contempt—and slammed a fist into one of the partitions as he lunged out.

"You've implicated Judge McGuire as having a connection to the victims," the mayor continued.

"*Implicate* is a strong word," Kate said smoothly. "I expressed my concern for Judge McGuire's safety."

"If Cole McGuire was doing his job, the city wouldn't be playing host to a madman."

"The chief and I are doing all we can to prevent another attack." Kate kept her voice level.

"If not for the chief, San Domingo wouldn't have a conspiracy on its hands."

"That's not fair," she said, sounding cold. "Nothing about this meeting has been fair. Impromptu meetings can be dangerous. Chief McGuire deserves to be heard. Especially since you're linking his name to a conspiracy."

His eyes narrowed. But before the mayor could proceed, Cole emerged from behind a partition. His face was devoid of all expression.

"What conspiracy?" Cole asked. He faced his accuser with dark, piercing eyes.

"I was just discussing your future with Agent Quin, Chief."

"No one told me you were looking for me," Cole said.

"Spur-of-the-moment decision. As soon as I heard you'd allowed another attack, I thought it was high time I put you back in line. Call it gut instinct, but I'm not satisfied with the direction this investigation is taking."

Every face in the room was directed at Cole. Everyone waited attentively for an answer.

"Gut instinct?" Cole snapped. "I'll tell you what I call it. I call it bureaucratic manipulation. Politics!"

"Don't raise your voice to me, McGuire. I'm not above losing my patience with you. With an investigation in as sorry shape as this one is, you can't afford to antagonize a man in my position."

"That sounds like a threat, Mayor. You want to go on record with it? I can have the press here inside five minutes."

Kate stiffened when she saw Cole's jaw go rigid. The tips of his ears were beet red, but still he eyed the mayor with a guarded expression.

Tense and alert, she considered the mayor's vindictive machinations. The observation caused an uncomfortable ache inside her. She'd provided him with a weapon to point at Cole.

"You need a scapegoat for your three-ring circus," Cole added.

"Now wait a minute!" the mayor shouted, his anger reverberating off the walls. "You're out of line!"

"No, *you're* out of line, Mayor. And I'm here to warn you that your tourist-minded intentions and your elected position don't allow you the luxury of getting involved in a police investigation. They'll only get in the way, slow things down, confuse people."

"The only one confused here is you!" The mayor's eyes narrowed with blistering ire as he faced Cole. "You're not indispensable, McGuire. Not to anyone. Remember that."

"Good of you to swing by," Cole said.

"That sounds like a dismissal, Chief. I've hardly gotten started here."

"Reporters are waiting outside for your statement, Your Honor," said one of the mayor's aides who'd just appeared.

Kate stood aside, stunned, as Cole ground his teeth and struggled not to hit the man. But before Cole had time to act, the mayor had moved across the floor and was on his way out the door. He paused briefly to speak again.

"I don't have to elaborate on what kind of problem this is for the city. I want this wrapped up as soon as possible. I've authorized all the overtime you'll need. I want Agent Quin kept abreast. Access to your squad meetings, all the files, any developments—as they come in. The works."

Kate watched Cole open his mouth to protest and then close it again.

The mayor turned to her. "You've given me new hope, Agent Quin. Our meeting proved to be very illuminating." Mayor Madden's expression was patronizing as he turned and left. Scoot slipped out behind him.

"Damn you," she whispered to the mayor as the implications of his words became clear in her mind.

Cole turned to leave, too.

"Wait," she pleaded. "Let me explain."

"Explain what? This isn't so difficult to understand." His tone was as dead as the look in his eyes. "You crossed the line, Kate."

His words chilled her like a cold hand squeezing her heart.

"No—you're mistaken about that."

"I don't want to talk anymore," Cole said.

"Then will you listen?" she demanded, unwilling to give up. "It's important for you to hear what I have to say."

A full minute elapsed before Cole responded. "I've already heard enough."

Rifling through the heap of files on her desk, she fished out the brown envelope and pushed it into Cole's hand.

"Then read these pages," she said urgently. "They'll explain a great deal to you—there may be something here. Something important. See what you think. If you agree, call me in Wickenburg."

That got his attention. A look of alarm flashed in his eyes. "What is it?"

Kate stared at him as the implications of her discovery became clear in her mind. "I'm not certain yet, but let's say that the odds of a breakthrough just dropped from one in a million—to one in a thousand."

THE URGE TO EMBRACE HER surged through Cole. Maybe she wouldn't forgive him for allowing today's briefing to take a demoralizing turn. Maybe she wouldn't ever find the strength in her heart to trust him. Maybe he would never be happy again.

Damn the maybes in his life. Beginning with Kate, he was taking charge of those maybes—because the thought of allowing himself to lose her again sent a convulsive shiver through his body. Existence wasn't enough for Cole. Not anymore. Floating through each day with the real purpose missing from his life, was worse than confronting his fear of rejection from her.

"We can't afford the time of dividing our efforts," he said. What seemed like eternity stretched between them.

He thought of her fragile state earlier. He'd left her open and vulnerable, to face his men. He'd tried to keep a professional distance, to allow her to do her job. He'd never intended to alienate her. Nor did he intend to banish her from his life—again.

"I owe you an apology, Kate."

"Thanks," she said softly. "Accepted."

"Now, then," she continued, the professional again, "we need to talk."

As excitement mounted in Kate's expression, Cole couldn't help smiling. "My office—"

"No," she cut in. "Not here."

"The cottage?"

She nodded. "We've just been dealt a wild card on the investigation."

"Good. We need all the luck we can get."

For the first time in months, Cole felt euphoric.

Chapter Seven

Kate's euphoria was short-lived. Before she had the chance to savor her silent victory with Cole, her heart had plunged to her stomach.

Outside the police station, an attractive redhead in a gleaming limousine gestured to Cole.

"Who is she?" Kate asked, while a surge of ridiculous jealousy swept over her.

Cole blinked, his only reaction to her demand.

She involuntarily hugged herself against a chill creeping over her, and it had nothing to do with the temperature outside. Her mood at once turned foul. Not even the fresh night air could improve it as she watched the woman motion Cole over to the car. She gave Kate a tight little smile, then turned her full attention to Cole. From the back seat of the limo, the woman sat waiting, very still, and very determined.

"Excuse me for a minute, Kate," Cole said, his gaze fixed on the redhead.

She nodded, chagrined by his detachment. For all that she knew Cole, she failed to read the emotion in his eyes. Nor was she prepared for Scoot's sudden appearance.

"She's a looker, ain't she?" he drawled.

"It's the clothes," Kate said, jealousy nudging at her self-control. "And formaldehyde."

"Ouch!"

Kate couldn't begin to think why she should bother being upset. She'd done her very best, and she'd convinced Cole to listen to her. "Do you know who she is?" Kate asked, without taking her eyes from the redhead.

Of course you do. Partners knew everything, more than they would ever tell. It was some sort of code of honor between them.

"Everybody knows her," he said matter-of-factly.

"Never mind," Kate said. "I'm not interested."

"You will be."

Kate glared at the loyal detective, and he clammed up. For about two seconds.

"Rumor has it you two were friendly," he plowed on. "Not that I give a damn."

"I didn't figure you for a gossip."

Unaffected, he persisted. "You two still friends?"

"Sworn enemies."

Scoot quickly put his smile away when he saw Cole motioning him over to the limo.

"Excuse me a minute," the detective said to Kate.

"Right," she mumbled after he'd moved off.

She was about to do the same. Leave. But there was the small problem of wheels. All she needed was one more look at Cole standing on the curb, lounging against the limo. Her stomach turned over, and she started walking back inside headquarters to call for a rental car.

"Want a ride home?" came a familiar voice.

Scoot was back, and she forced a smile.

"That's definitely a consideration."

Unexpectedly, he stopped and looked at her. "You okay?"

"Why do you ask?"

She wasn't offended, although she considered oversolicitous behavior a terminal disease. But she realized his concern was genuine.

"You look kinda pale."

"Jet lag, that's all. I'm all right."

Kate squeezed out the words, feeling as though she'd been kicked in the stomach. She could sense the detective's eyes boring into her, and only then did she realize that the limo was pulling away from the curb, and that Cole was gone. As in vanished. He'd committed his disappearing act with the waxen-faced redhead. All Kate could do was stand there and gawk.

"Good," Scoot said, inappropriately cheery. His tone said he didn't believe her, but he showed her a mouth overcrowded with teeth, anyway.

She lifted one hand in a gesture of frustration and uncertainty. Damned if she was going to allow jealousy to make her vulnerable to Cole McGuire. But they had to talk about the Judge—and soon. There was always the possibility that he could be in danger.

"Can we go?" she asked.

"You like hamburgers?"

"Love them."

His teeth flashed. "That's good. I was afraid maybe you ate every third day or something. Come on," he said. "I'm parked two cars over."

"How do you feel about a fed picking your brain?"

"As long as you leave something for me, be my guest."

Kate hadn't realized that Scoot had been holding her arm until the moment he released it. She followed him to his car and he unlocked the door on the passenger side. She slid inside, leaned back in the seat, and watched him stroll around the brown "bomb" to the driver's side and fold himself into the seat. He was thick and stubby, not really overweight, just squatty with ample flesh. She considered his thoughtfulness, and decided he might have some redeeming qualities, after all. She could use a friend. Even if he was Cole's partner.

"What happened back there—it ain't nothing to get upset over."

"What happened back there doesn't concern me," Kate said, trying harder to convince herself of that. "What does concern me is how I'm going to get to Wickenburg."

"I just thought you might like to know why he vamoosed like he did."

The redhead wasn't your garden-variety date, but Kate had the picture, and she didn't need Scoot to color it in for her. She was already hurting enough.

"The chief says—"

"You're to drive me home?" Kate finished, taking a calculated guess. It was easy enough to figure out.

"That's right," he told her. "It ain't that far. Twenty minutes, tops. My set of wheels rides like a cloud. Hey? You listening?"

Scoot was direct to a fault, always wanting a face pointed at him. The act was wearying, but she was beginning to like him in spite of it. She nodded, and he resumed talking.

"How 'bout I brief you on my theory about the case while I'm driving."

Do I have a choice? "Swell," she said.

Scoot headed north on Castle Avenue while Kate admonished herself for the childish attack of jealousy. More important, she needed to talk to Cole. Fill him in on the conspiracy angle before the mayor got to him about it. Scoot pulled into the first fast-food restaurant to dot the highway. The five o'clock dinner rush had formed a long line at the drive-through window.

"Hamburgers and fries coming up," he said, and got out of the car.

Food. Caffeine. And Cole's right-hand man. Perfect. She gave him a thumbs-up. He'd managed to make the hurt easier to bear. Kate was thankful for the diversion.

And Scoot was right about the car. It looked like the remains of a World War II tank, but it rode like a dream.

She'd barely had time to peruse the parking lot when she spotted Scoot lumbering back to the car.

"Thanks," she murmured, then sorted through the sacks he handed her.

"Scoot," she said, surprised that she'd addressed him by his name for the first time since she'd met him. "Did you accompany the victim to the emergency room?"

"I didn't hold her hand or nothing, but, yeah, I rode down with her."

"You bagged her clothes?" Kate asked, slipping straws into their drinks.

"What is this, twenty questions? Yeah. I had an officer carry them to the lab."

"All right then, Detective," Kate said when they were on their way again, "regale me with your theory. I'm all ears."

She crammed a hamburger into her mouth and munched. She wasn't in the mood to talk, anyway.

"All this fuss," Scoot said, with no compassion, "when it would be just as well if our angel of mercy croaked."

"You think it's an error of judgment to help the victims of a crime?" Kate asked.

Scoot shook his head emphatically. "I'm only talking about the evil ones. They don't deserve help."

The evil ones? The words rose and fell around Kate as she mentally devoured them. It was an unusual way to view the victims. She wondered whether to thank Scoot or suspect him. He had drawn the first line in the psychological sketch. And it was an uncannily accurate one.

"That's a judgment you shouldn't be making," Kate said, straightening defensively.

She figured too many years on the force predisposed him to bias. But a lot could be gleaned from a good friend and partner.

Chapter Eight

Scoot waved and drove off without getting out of the "bomb." Kate had given him an exercise to make him happy. With the look of a cat with a mouse under its paw, the C of D had agreed to pull the police reports on each of the victims. Kate was interested in any similarities in their crimes and arrests.

Fatigue gnawed at her like a hungry vulture. And she had that flat feeling. She needed to lift her spirits before she went down to see the McGuires. Exercise usually worked. A swim sounded good. It had been much too cool the evening before. She peered around the corner of the cottage to have a look at the pool.

Libby McGuire was breaststroking the length of the water, first one way, then the other. Swimming had always been part of her daily routine.

Kate strolled down the patio steps. She watched as Libby's solid body propelled itself through the water like a sleek fish. Libby's appreciable height had landed her a modeling career as a young woman—something she had given up to devote her life to her family. Kate had to admit, it had always been a comforting thought to know that Libby was readily available.

When Libby spotted Kate, she sidestroked to the edge of the pool and pulled herself up the ladder as Kate extended her terry-cloth robe to her. Libby embraced Kate in much the same way a mother would a daughter.

"Kate, dear," she murmured, in that familiar deep, soothing voice. "Welcome home."

"Thank you," Kate managed to whisper.

"Now, then, let's have a look at you," Libby said, drawing back, with a smile.

She was a vivacious woman in her late forties, with cropped brown hair sprinkled with gray, keenly intelligent eyes, a handsome face, and a quick smile. But she had aged sufficiently to distract Kate.

"Tell me everything," Libby began. "All about the trip, your job, how you like Quantico, what's going on in your life."

You did not chat with Libby McGuire. You listened. She was a compulsive talker. She didn't bother to remove the oversize shades she was wearing. Kate spotted the wound on her face, anyway—a faint contusion under one eye, puffed like a ripe plum.

"What happened to you?" Kate asked.

"You wouldn't believe me if I told you," Libby said, laughing.

"Still sleepwalking?"

"That's what the Judge tells me." She brushed at the purplish mass. "These crimes," she continued, shaking her head. "A terrible thing to happen to San Domingo."

Kate nodded, but said nothing. She felt far too edgy right now to surrender to the mystery of the murders.

"Do you think there will be more?"

Kate pressed her lips together, attempting to buy time. She would not insult Libby's mental capabilities with anything less than the truth.

"I practically guarantee it," she said flatly.

"A pity."

"We've got 3.5 victims—"

"What?"

"Didn't you know? The latest victim survived the attack."

Libby's face blanched. She squeezed her eyes shut for a moment. "Thank God," she muttered, visibly shaken. "The Judge said—he thought she had died."

"He isn't blaming himself?" Kate asked.

"I don't know," Libby mumbled, looking toward the house below.

Though Kate felt anxious, she was deliberately slow about responding, not wanting to say anything to upset Libby, who must have known the victim had been a defendant in her husband's court.

"He really needs you right now," Kate said to her. "Are you up to it?"

For a moment, Libby averted her eyes and glanced, instead, at the bright pink bougainvilleas cascading from their hanging pots, announcing the arrival of spring. Then her face brightened.

"Of course. Come down to the house, see the Judge."

Kate nodded, and a grin pushed Libby's face into a series of creases and lines.

"Is this visit to be construed as a reunion?" Cole's mother asked, lifting an eyebrow.

"You never give up," Kate said, returning the smile while secretly examining the notion.

IT WAS AFTER TEN WHEN Kate returned to the cottage. The door was unlocked, and she stepped inside and kicked off her shoes. With only the moonlight to guide her, she shed her holster and weapon, and placed them on the coffee table. Next she shimmied out of the binding jeans. She tossed them across the room and began stripping off the rest of her clothes as she went, heading straight for the bathroom to have a long soak in a hot tub.

The cottage wasn't lavishly decorated, but it was quaint and clean. Moonlight streamed through the bathroom window, allowing her an opportunity to search for soap and towels. She found them, then sat down on the side of the tub to pull back the shower curtain. When she did, rising steam from the already filled tub first gave her a start, then caressed her face.

Kate stiffened. She felt a chill at the base of her spine. She went for her gun. It was in the living room, right where she'd left it. Unnerved, naked except for bikini panties and bra, she then returned to the bedroom to have a closer look. A lump moved on the bed, and Kate felt her blood run cold. She inched backward toward the bathroom. The lump moved again, causing a surge of fear to shoot through Kate's stomach, and she raised her gun in both hands.

"I didn't mean to scare you," a familiar voice floated up from the bed.

She expelled a heavy sigh as she placed the weapon on a dresser.

"Damn you, Cole. I could have shot you."

"Is that any way to say hello?"

She stood in the bathroom doorway, too shaken to move. She wanted to go to him, put her arms around him. He held out his hand...but there was the redhead.

"Go away," she said, with all the calm she could manage while her heart was slamming against her rib cage.

Like a sleek cat, Cole lifted his lithe body from the bed and was moving toward her before she could slither out of his reach.

"Kate, I need to talk to you."

His deft hands were on her shoulders, working, massaging, moving downward until they were cupping her breasts as intimately as her bra was.

"That's what telephones are for," she whispered, mortified at her body's response.

Instantly, she was ready for him, and she couldn't do a damn thing to stop it.

"About tonight." His voice had turned husky.

"I didn't say I was interested." Her voice sounded shaky, her breath was irregular. "Did I say that?"

"Not yet," he replied, still molding her will as well as her body with his quick hands. "But you are."

She wanted to argue that point. Tell him otherwise. But the wrenching truth was that he was right.

"The information is not a professional necessity," she whispered, fighting a growing hunger for him.

"Oh, but it is."

His busy hands were momentarily still, and she gasped audibly as he withdrew them. Now was her chance to break the spell. She tried to push him away. No use. Her heart wasn't in it.

"You really don't know what this is about," he said.

"Keep going," Kate said, putting an indifferent look on her face. There had to be some way to hide the emotion welling up inside her. Damn him. He was amused, and she was coming apart inside. "You might hit on something I'll buy. Though I doubt it."

"Okay, partner," he said, bracing his arms against the wall on either side of her, effectively trapping her with his body. "That is, if we're still partners."

"Why wouldn't we be?" she asked demurely, certain she felt his pounding heart thumping against her breast.

Any second she was going to act on impulse. She wanted to feel his naked body next to hers. She wanted him inside her.

Abruptly, she stiffened.

"What is it?" Cole asked. "What's the matter?"

She'd glanced at the brown envelope lying on the bedside table. Reality impinged on the best feeling she'd had in eighteen months: she *had* to talk to Cole about the Judge....

"Tonight had nothing to do with you—or the case," he murmured in a deep voice while he gently pressed a knee between her legs. "It's just something I had to work out."

She gasped, realizing she was almost at the point of no return. Recovery was probably out of the question now.

"Please, spare me the sordid details of your private life. Really, I'm not interested."

Liar.

"Did Scoot explain anything at all to you?" Cole asked.

"No more than I'm going to allow you to explain," she said in a voice that was heating up.

"You're jealous," he said, amused again. He lifted his head to stare down at her intently.

"Nonsense." Her voice belied her retort.

He shifted his knee and watched for her reaction. Sensations collided inside her while he exerted more pressure with each stroke of his leg. Who was she punishing by not giving in?

"We have to talk," she said.

"I think otherwise," he whispered, lowering his head to kiss her neck.

"No."

"Okay—I'll explain first."

"You've nothing to ex—"

"The attorney general," Cole murmured into her ear, his breathing ragged.

"What are you talking about?"

"The redhead in the limo—she's Millicent Finney—attorney general."

Kate rolled her eyes. When the realization hit her full force, she stiffened, then pushed Cole away. "You mean that you and the AG are—"

"No," he said, still in a husky tone. "Nothing like that."

"Damn you—how could you leave me standing there like that?"

"I was concerned that you'd get the wrong idea about her, what she wanted with me. She owed me a favor. I called it in tonight."

"You called her?"

"The mayor wants to sit second chair on this investigation," he said in one breath. "I haven't dated since you left," he said in another.

Kate pressed a finger to his lips. "I don't want to share this moment with a haughty redhead or a hostile mayor."

"Come here," Cole murmured, in his deepest voice.

Kate slid into his arms, molding herself to his rigid body. "Cole, I want to ask you something."

"Hmm?"

"You knew with the second one that this was the work of a psychopath, didn't you?"

"I knew after the fiftieth wannabe killer had called in his confession. Just like the other forty-nine callers, he didn't know about the lividity, or the cause of death, either. We've managed to keep that out of the papers—that somebody out there gets his kicks from hanging corpses."

"Did you consider phoning me after that call?"

After a moment Cole looked at her. It was as though she'd pushed a button, the wrong one.

"I can't remember how many times I've considered calling you during the past year and a half."

"Why didn't you?" she asked bravely.

"I was too busy hoping that the phone would *ring.*"

For the first time in so many months, Kate felt relief. The feeling overwhelmed her. They had continued to care for each other a great deal; they just hadn't gotten around to trusting each other.

"I want to make love to you, Kate."

"No," she said as her uneasiness grew. "You want to prove that you can."

"I already know what I can do. I want your consent. I want to hear the same thing from you."

"What?"

"You can't be surprised."

In truth, he was right. They had made their fiercest love during emotional highs such as this one. His eyes were wary, as if he were familiar with the tightrope he was walking right now.

"Making love to you was always better when you were angry."

He was right again. She tried to summon up her courage, her strength, even her earlier indignation—anything to help her resist six-feet-plus of rock-hard body pressing against her and tempting her to do something she knew she would live to regret.

"You're blushing," he said, as if the observation incriminated her.

"I'm just working up a sweat. A good case always does that to me."

"Kate..."

"A good case...makes life worth living," she almost whispered, wanting to sound indifferent, but failing miserably.

One last time, Kate rationalized. She would make love with him one last time—because after that, she would have to tell him about the Judge. After that, she didn't know what was going to happen. Would he understand that she was only trying to do her job?

"I've missed you," he said softly, with his lips pressed against first one closed eye, then the other.

Cole slid his arms around her, unhooked her bra and slipped it from her shoulders. Her generous breasts spilled out as if protesting their prior restraint, and the lacy undergarment fell to the floor. Tenderly, cautiously, his strong hands cupped them, and Kate felt overwhelmed by the mounting sensations coming to life inside her.

"You've missed me, too," he told her.

Only his rapid breathing belied his control. She hooked her hands around his neck, molding herself into his arms as he lifted her to the bed. If this was really the end, she wasn't going out of his life without one last, shared intimacy.

"Damn you," she said, her voice wobbling as she choked back a sob.

She clung to him, her face pressed into his shoulder, as he lowered her onto the bed.

"Think of the reality of things," she mumbled, losing fast to temptation.

He began to move against her, in slow, deliberate movements, designed to draw out the animal in her.

"Reality can wait until tomorrow," he said brokenly. "We deserve tonight."

If she made love with him, Kate knew, and if she wanted more than this night with him, he could reject and alienate her with a suddenness and viciousness that would leave her stunned again. And when he was gone, when she was alone, she would be crushed by the loss and would learn to hate herself as she had never done before. Still, right now, she wanted nothing in the world more than Cole's arms around her, his body close to hers, his breath mingling with hers. Him filling her.

"After all," he said gently, "this will only be a few stolen moments."

"Sometimes I think that's all there are—stolen moments. And dreams."

What had seemed important five minutes earlier, blurred; she was willing to risk everything for a night with him.

"The trick is to recognize the stolen moments." He put his hand to her face, stroking away the hot, salty tears. "To take them when you can."

She closed her eyes, tried to stop the tears, but they ran across her cheeks, into her hair, onto Cole's face as he held her close.

"We have tonight," she whispered.

There was no hesitation on Cole's part. He stood to shrug out of his clothes while Kate lay watching. His body was as close to perfect as any woman could hope for, and for the next few hours, he belonged to her.

"No regrets?" he murmured, lowering himself over her.

"No regrets," she said softly, blinking away the sudden onslaught of fresh tears.

No shame, and no guilt. She couldn't deny her urges. Need took over as she submitted to it, fully aware that he wouldn't disappoint. He entered her in one swift motion, making her whole again, making them one. She heard a faint sob slide from his throat.

"Do you have any idea how good you feel?" he murmured.

"Show me," she whispered.

In her desperate need for all of him, her hands tugged to draw him closer, her legs wrapped around him and held on as each thrust escalated her desire for him to an all-time high. But she couldn't hold on for much longer. There was no time for teasing, for tempting. His strokes deepened, quickened, until she convulsed around him in tight, rapid, spasms. The overwhelming pleasure heightened as she felt his body tense, then go rigid in her arms, before finally he collapsed against her. And then Kate luxuriated in the feel of Cole's body next to hers. If only for a little while, they were together again. Beyond this moment, nothing else mattered.

Kate was wrapped in a towel that revealed enough of everything to distract Cole. Only now she was all business, and Cole elected to dismiss his less-than-honorable intentions. He handed her a glass of juice and thought about how she had wrapped herself around him last night.

"Did I wake you?" he murmured as his lips brushed her ear.

"The next best thing," she said, heading toward the bedroom again to dress. "I smelled coffee brewing."

"Omelet's ready," he called out a few moments later.

When she reappeared, she was slipping an oversize powder-blue sweater over her black unitard. He considered how much he liked her straight from the shower, without makeup, hair still wet, face pink from a thorough scrub. There was a vulnerability about her that provoked feelings he hadn't experienced in a long time.

He joined her at the table.

"This is good, McGuire," she said, stabbing at the omelet with her fork. "We have to talk," she told him between bites.

When she'd finished eating and was sipping coffee, a frown slowly lodged between her brows. She leaned forward. "I'm worried about the Judge."

"The *Judge?*"

She nodded.

Jumping right to the point was nothing new for Kate, once she had everything in place. And once she had everything in place, she was usually right in her calculations. But because he was a man who took his time, watched his footing, Cole leaned back and thought about what he'd heard.

"He's fine, Kate. Tired, tense, overworked, but his job is everything to him. You know that. These killings have all of us concerned."

"That's not exactly what I meant."

"What do you mean?"

"I can link the Judge to the homicides, right here in these reports."

"What the hell is that supposed to mean?"

"His job is part of the problem, but not in the way you're thinking." She paused, as though to consider what she was about to tell him. She struggled with it, then said, finally, "I think the Judge is the common denominator in these murders."

"Kate, you're not making any sense. I know he dismissed Phyllis Coffer's case shortly before the attack but—"

"Each victim shared something in common. Your dad tried and adjudicated all of their cases. And he cut them all loose because of loopholes in the legal system."

No leap of faith was required to buy her theory. It was a scenario Cole preferred not to contemplate.

"Dammit, Kate. You're taking this too far if you're hanging around hoping to find a glimpse of impropriety."

She was quiet for a moment. But there could be no mistake. Cole hadn't failed to see that fleeting doubt in her eyes. He saw a thread of potential intrigue emerging. He felt his pulse rate climb as he leaned forward to listen.

"Maybe you're too close to this," she murmured while her frown deepened.

That possibility gave birth to an uncomfortable ache inside him. He was teetering on the edge.

"Think about it," she said. He did. "These murder victims weren't randomly chosen. The killer carefully selected each one of them, and they all met the same identical criteria. Each faced felony charges in Judge McGuire's court. He freed each one of them on a technicality."

"You're suggesting that some psychopath is systematically purging the dregs of society because the system failed?"

"It's a possibility we can't rule out."

Alarm came first. What about his dad's safety? Half wild with fear, he caught her by the arm. "Do you know what you're saying?"

"Read the reports."

For the next half hour, Cole pored over them. They—and Kate's certainty—convinced him. He no longer thought the killer chose his victims randomly. No, there was a pattern. Now he was certain of it. Chilling. All the victims had been caught up in the legal system. All were free to continue their atrocious activities after his dad had released them.

"All right," he said quietly, "interrogate him."

"I don't want to interrogate him," Kate said defensively. "I just want the truth."

"So do I, dammit. No one wants the truth more than I do. No one. But my father is not involved—" His words braked to a sudden stop as a thought slammed into his mind. "For God's sake, Kate. You're not accusing the Judge?"

She stiffened. "I'm sharing information with you, that's all," she said, when the shrill ring of the telephone was heard.

Cole continued to brood while he sipped his coffee.

"Scoot," Kate explained, hanging up the receiver and sending him an unreadable glance. "The search warrant for the victim's house is signed and waiting for us."

They did not speak as they placed dishes in the sink and prepared to leave.

Cole pulled the cottage door shut behind him, wishing he could shake the uneasy feeling that things weren't ever going to be the same again.

Chapter Nine

Kate had made a promise to herself to leave last night far behind. In spite of that, however, her thoughts were engaged in a fierce debate.

"I am sorry," Cole murmured as he drove toward San Domingo. "I shouldn't have jumped to a conclusion about your intentions like that."

Kate couldn't say it was all right, because it wasn't. "You're free to do and say what you want."

"The truth is, I get stingy about what I want." His low, husky voice caressed her. "I'm finding it damn hard not to want you."

His eyes appeared bluer as he studied her for a reaction. Kate willed her emotions not to respond. But she couldn't pretend there weren't a thousand obstacles between them, even though they both might wish otherwise. Regret was paramount in her heart as she spoke.

"If we're going to work together," she began, "I think it would be best if we maintained a professional distance."

"Why are you so hung up on this 'professional' business?"

Kate rolled her eyes at him. Self-preservation was one answer. "Because we've got a job to do," she said, giving him another.

"If that's how you want things."

She wanted to answer yes—she needed to—but she couldn't. All she could do was nod. Their gazes met and clung. Warmth spread over Kate's cheeks. Cole narrowed his eyes for a beat, then nodded briskly himself.

"Thank you," she said.

"All in a day's work."

An apology was on the tip of her tongue.

"Still don't trust yourself with me?" he asked. "I made less of an impression on you last night than I'd hoped."

"Let's stick to the matter at hand, shall we?" she responded quietly. She had developed a pounding headache from lack of sleep. Her blood-sugar level was fluctuating. She fished inside her purse until she found a roll of candy. It was a quick fix, but it would have to do.

"I thought we *were* discussing the matter at hand. My mistake. Where do we start?"

"Start with the victims," she said. "Let's review everything we know about them."

Cole was one of those rare men who couldn't be pressured. He did his own thinking, set his own pace, refused to be bullied. Kate took comfort in those qualities. At times his reticence was an affront to those around him. But Kate respected his tolerance for listening. He was well-grounded, and it gave her a sense of security, of strength.

He started at the beginning, with the first victim, and for the next few miles, worked his way forward. Kate relaxed and listened.

"She was a nurse," he said of the most recent victim. "She worked in the intensive care unit of Sun City Hospital."

"What happened?"

"Four months ago, news broke about some of her patients dying mysteriously. Day before yesterday a sequestered jury sent word to the Judge that they'd been unable to reach a decision in her trial."

"Go on."

"The Judge made a blistering decision to declare a mistrial." Cole gripped the wheel and glanced at her as he spoke. "He dismissed the case without prejudice, cut Phyllis Coffer loose about an hour before she was attacked."

Kate sat quietly, absorbing and processing information. Cole drove in silence, his expression enigmatic.

"That puts a new spin on things," Kate remarked finally in a quiet, meditative voice. "Maybe Scoot has a point." A chill raced up her spine. If she had any doubts as to the reality of this situation, they were gone now. "There's no honor or moral rectitude to be upheld here."

"How does that translate?"

"None of the victims have been persons of absolute integrity." Kate was beginning to understand Scoot's harsh analysis. Maybe it didn't have anything to do with being cynical. "All had sordid, pathetic pasts. That's the first link. But I'm convinced that the link to the killer lies within the court's adjudication process."

Cole stared at her with dread in his eyes.

"So we're talking revenge as a motive here?" he asked.

"Revenge might not be definitive. I think the symbolic nature of the crimes might indicate a 'save the world' complex."

"From what?"

"Evil."

There had been no pattern to the time frame between killings, except that, as the killer's frustration escalated, the time frame narrowed. And Kate understood that the acceleration of his acts might prevent them from rescuing the next victim.

"No offense," Cole said, "but you're beginning to sound like Scoot."

She gave him one of her looks, then fell silent, considering this brand-new particle of information that had dislodged itself. She looked over and caught Cole flashing her a lopsided grin so charming that it twisted something painfully in her chest.

"What?" she asked. "Why are you looking at me so?"

"I like watching you process information," he murmured. "Figure out anything?"

"I haven't yet, unless you're interested in theories."

"Everybody has a theory." He faced the road once more, showing her a strong profile. "When you start taking them seriously, they diffuse the effort."

Kate had determination. And she'd never wanted so badly to have another person believe in her skills. But she'd broken a cardinal rule by letting herself get emotionally involved; in doing so she lost whatever control she'd had of the situation. She knew what she had to do to retrieve it.

"Why don't you tell me why you're so certain I have nothing constructive to offer to this investigation," she said abruptly.

His expression softened. "You haven't asked."

"I'm asking now."

"You're a mind hunter," he pointed out. "You may find him on paper, but you're no more apt to spot him across a crowded room than I am."

As they regarded each other warily, the silence once more grew strained.

Cole eased the tension when he said, "We'll get him, but first a couple of things have to happen."

"All right," she said in her most professional tone of voice. "I'm listening."

"One, we find evidence we've overlooked."

"That's a good start."

"Two, he keeps on until he botches things, or the intended victim survives the attack to identify him."

She listened cautiously, but without protest. Cole went on to speculate about whether Phyllis Coffer would regain consciousness with all her faculties intact—about whether she would regain consciousness at all.

"Meantime, we have zero on the big screen," she said. "The way I see things, that leaves you needing my help."

"I admire your enthusiasm," he replied. "But there's more to solving this case than boring into someone's head and matching wits there."

"Is that how you see it? No wonder you act as though I've ganged up on you with the enemy." She stated her case. "We have someone making up the rules as he kills. It might help to understand what makes him tick."

"I can't argue with that."

Of all the remarks Kate had expected from him, that one was the least likely. She took a deep breath and savored the flood of relief surging through her.

"Just promise me one thing," he said.

Kate glanced at him, preparing herself for a belated disclaimer to his sudden leap of faith.

"What's that?" she asked.

"Don't forget whose side you're on."

Yet another time, Cole had surprised her.

COLE WATCHED AS A SWEET smile parted Kate's lips, a charming sign of surrender in her. The rich, delicious scent of her fragrance was in the air.

They had just reached the San Domingo city limits. He gave her a sidelong glance. Without makeup, there was a purity about her that he admired. The powder-blue sweater dress she wore looked sophisticated. He allowed his gaze to drift to the generous swell of her breasts—and discovered that the fires from last night's lovemaking still burned.

"You won't regret it," she was saying. "You'll be surprised at what the crime scene will have to say to you about the offender."

"I'd prefer to extract my information from the surviving victim, but . . . I'll take a look at your profile," he said with as much nonchalance as he could muster. "It's not an endorsement, or a commitment, or anything like that."

"No, of course not," Kate replied, growing meditative for the moment.

From McCarrol Road, Cole turned north onto Seventy-fifth Avenue. Predominately two-story homes nestled in the foothills where streets curved and looped around bright green golf courses surrounding man-made lakes—a strange sight smack in the middle of the desert. The victim's house was part of a high-priced subdivision called Desert Lakes, not the sort of area in which one would have expected crime or criminals.

"These invisible loops and whorls might provide you with the blueprint of a killer," he admitted, "but I'd trade them all for a set of physical fingerprints covering a crime scene."

"Uh-hmm," she murmured. "I doubt he'll give that up to you." She sank back against the car seat, biting at her full lower lip.

"You make it sound as though he litters by design."

"He's ego driven. If I'm right, he's been playing with us—tossing out minute crumbs to keep us interested."

"We've done everything except to X-ray the crime scenes. We're coming up empty."

"Maybe you've been looking too hard." Kate turned her intense gaze on Cole. "Remember, he's very cunning."

"That's the house," Cole said, nodding his head toward the right-hand side of the quiet street. "The one where the brown 'bomb' landed."

At once Kate's attention was drawn to Scoot, planted at the victim's front door like a sentry on duty.

"The city ought to condemn that car," Cole added. "He could have a county-issued car, but he refuses one."

"I rode home in the 'bomb' last night. Between new shocks and a recent tune-up, the car rides like a dream."

Cole studied Kate through narrowed eyes.

"More like a bad dream," he grumbled. "I doubt he'd admit to how often it breaks down." He redirected the conversation. "You ready to start digging?"

"I've always wanted to discover buried treasure."

Cole grinned. "Now you're getting into the spirit of this."

The next moment the Caprice belched out a backfire and promptly died, leaving Cole to force-steer the white "boat" into the driveway next to the brown "bomb."

KATE ADMIRED THE battered brown Oldsmobile sedan cooling its wheels in Phyllis Coffer's driveway as Cole coasted in to park beside it, mud cakes and all. Without a word, Cole climbed out of his beloved Caprice and slammed the door.

"County issue?" Kate asked, patting the white hood of the Caprice.

He nodded, tongue in cheek and brow furrowed. But there was no mistaking the grin tugging at his mouth.

"I smell gas," Cole said. "It's probably the damn fuel pump."

"Carburetor needs adjusting," Kate muttered as she headed across the lawn toward the front door. "Face it, McGuire, I know more about cars than you do." She glanced back at him to finish with a knowing grin, "Always have."

"Duty calls, *compadres,*" Scoot said in greeting. "What kept you?"

"Don't blame it on the car," Kate chided.

"Looks like nurses must make more dough than cops," Scoot observed.

It was eleven forty-five, a full hour since he had called Wickenburg with news of obtaining the search warrant. Kate had known the instant she had spotted Scoot, that the detective had already been inside.

"Yeah," Cole growled, "that's because they earn their money."

"Which probably allows them to afford cars that run," Kate murmured.

"Whaddaya think, Kate?" Scoot broke in, his resonant voice booming.

"Depends on what you found inside."

Scoot raised his eyebrows at her. He reddened, but he stayed calm. She hoped he wouldn't bring up the Judge.

"I tried the door." He wiggled his eyebrows. "She's the trusting sort. Leaves the place unlocked."

After glancing at the determined detective, Kate knew that he hadn't been home all night. She noticed his soiled clothing—coffee-stained trousers, suit coat stiffened with grime—the same clothes he had worn yesterday. But his white shirt was bright and freshly laundered. He probably kept a supply in the trunk of his mud-caked Olds.

"Let's see the search warrant," Kate said.

"Don't you trust me?" Scoot challenged.

Kate wasn't about to blow any holes into this case in the event that it got to trial. She watched Scoot, waiting for an answer while the detective shuffled a rolled newspaper in his hands. He slapped his leg with it. Dust flew. Still Kate waited.

"Everybody should try reading the paper. It helps to broaden your horizons. Look here," he said too theatrically. Like a magician pulling a rabbit from a hat, Scoot pulled a folded document from inside the paper. "It's a search warrant."

He smiled broadly at Kate while she worked her hands into a pair of gloves. Cole and his chief detective began pulling on gloves, too. She wished Scoot would sit on his humor.

"Let's get this over with," Cole suggested, moving toward the front door.

"Let's peruse," Scoot said with sufficient enthusiasm to convince anybody that he was on his way inside Phyllis Coffer's home for the first time.

Kate rolled her eyes at Cole as his C of D flicked his hand at the door. It swung open.

The entrance hall separated a library from the kitchen, and led into an oversize living room with high ceilings. The library with its built-in bookshelves, was empty of books and furnishings. Glass-and-chrome furniture in the living room added to the cold, impersonal ambience.

"Like I said, nurses rake in more money than cops do."

At first glance, the house was immaculate, too clean, bordering on sterile.

"I'll check out her bedroom," Kate said.

"Me," the burly chief of detectives began, "I figure the refrigerator tells as much about how people live as any other part of the house."

The man had a point. Kate decided to follow him into the kitchen. Cole had the same inclination. The side-by-side, deluxe-model icebox offered up a half-full gallon container of cheap wine, moldy cheese, and a jar of green olives. Otherwise, the refrigerator was empty. The freezer housed a half-dozen frozen dinners and an unopened bag of crystal ice. The victim obviously found her pleasure someplace other than home.

"What do we have here?" Scoot asked.

He lifted a brochure off the kitchen countertop while his cigarette smoke swirled in the white beams of the overhead light fixture. Kate's eyes itched.

"Kill the cigarette, Scoot," Cole barked. "You know the rules."

The detective flicked his cigarette into the sink and ran water over it. It died slowly, sizzling and smelling terrible.

"'Ten easy steps to ensure safe and easy bankruptcy filings,'" Scoot read.

Kate abandoned the kitchen to check out the rest of the house, hoping to find evidence to tag. The place reminded her of a model home—nice, but cold, without roots, pictures, mementos. The guest room was as empty as the refrigerator. Only the master bedroom contained furniture.

She paused on the threshold to observe the room. There was a king-size bed with a white spread, white carpeting, a small desk, and a door that opened to a bath beyond. She went first to the desk.

Stacked neatly inside were all the usual envelopes, stationery, pens, pencils. One drawer had been reserved for way too many past-due notices on household bills. Kate found an answering machine on a nightstand. The red light was blinking. She rewound the messages—dozens, maybe. It appeared that Phyllis Coffer never erased them.

A few minutes of listening turned up nothing other than the usual hang-ups, computerized telemarketing solicitations, a lawn-mower service shop, and a video-rental call about overdue movies. The search warrant permitted the confiscation of certain materials, so Kate removed the tape and dropped it into a plastic bag. Next, she moved into the bathroom.

The medicine cabinet was a warehouse for a variety of drugs, the most potent of which was a vial of morphine. Phyllis Coffer had probably been helping herself to the hospital's supply.

"Doing any good?" Cole called out to her.

"Not much."

"What's that?" he asked when she returned to the kitchen.

"The tape from her answering machine." She dropped the plastic bag into her purse.

"Yeah?" Scoot drawled, his interest piqued. "Anything worth hearing?"

"I'm not sure yet. Apparently she never erased her messages. Tape's full," she said. "It'll take some time to sort it out. She had a small desk filled with past-due notices."

"What's in the other plastic bag?" Cole asked.

"A couple of empty glasses I found on a tray in the bathroom," Kate said. "I couldn't tell if they were clean and unused or empty and dirty."

"Anything else?" Cole prompted.

"The house is pin neat. But, under the surface, I found chaos. One of the desk drawers was a rat's nest of folders without labels, rubber bands, loose paper clips, bills, and unmarked medicine bottles."

"Anything there?"

"Nothing beyond the mess."

"What is it, Chief? The whole world gone nuts?"

Cole gave the question the shrug it deserved.

"Someone needs to canvas the neighborhood," Kate suggested. "Maybe she had enemies. She could have been getting threats and mentioned her fears to a neighbor."

"Scoot already has," Cole told her.

Kate looked to Scoot.

"Inconclusive," he said. "Nobody admitted to hearing or seeing anything. Nobody could recall seeing Phyllis Coffer during the past few days."

"Where's her car?" Kate asked. "The garage is empty."

"Impounded by the department," Cole replied.

Scoot shrugged. "What about it, Doc? Ain't we through here?"

Kate continued trying to iron out the wrinkles. "It might be a good idea for you to check out the car, Scoot, for a mobile telephone. If she has one, there will be a record of every call, in or out, local or long-distance."

"Been done. No phone," Scoot said shortly. "Hey, I'm hungry as hell."

Amused, Kate lifted a brow. "A public servant has to keep up his strength."

"The lady's got finesse," Cole murmured.

"You like baby back ribs?" The expression on Scoot's face told her that he was serious.

"I'll take you up on those another time," Kate said.

Scoot nodded and turned back to the subject at hand. "She lives normally enough. But our victim here must be one sick puppy."

"People who take lives usually are," Kate said.

"Twisted wiring," the C of D added, pointing a finger to his head. "Taking into account the Hangman, that makes two sick puppies. Hey, Doc, we almost got ourselves a litter."

Kate disliked hearing the killer referred to as the Hangman. It sounded flippant. She choked it down without saying anything.

"You're right about the wiring," Kate said. "And we simply are not able to do anything about crossed wires. Not yet, anyway."

"Lost cause," Scoot observed.

"There's always hope."

"Ain't that contrary to science?"

"We're not talking about science," Cole said.

"That's *all* we've talked about since she got here."

"If you're lucky," Cole chided, "maybe you'll learn something."

Kate felt the flash of admiration from Cole; she welcomed it. Admiration was easier to handle than the pain she'd been feeling.

"Later," Scoot said, sending them both a cocky smile. "I've got some real police work to do."

Kate and Cole walked him to the door, and from there watched him climb into his car.

"Hey, Doc," he called from the brown "bomb," "maybe we should do this again."

"Maybe." Kate hesitated for a moment, struggling with her thought. "The man's got an attitude," she confided to Cole. "But I like him."

"Don't be too hard on him. He's about three weeks away from permanent R and R."

"Since when does retirement make you defensive?"

"He's just jumpy. It's this whole serial-killer thing. Scoot is personalizing it. All three victims—and Phyllis Coffer—were his collars."

Chapter Ten

Kate swallowed that bite of information and processed it while Cole helped her into the car. He cranked the Caprice repeatedly, but it refused to start.

"You've flooded the carburetor."

"Anything else?" Cole asked.

"You're draining the battery. Let it sit a minute while we talk."

"Sounds serious," he said.

"Why did you withhold information from the investigation?"

That got his attention. Resentment washed over Cole's features, and his weary look was replaced by a brief flash of anger.

"Instinct is a major part of my job. If Scoot was showing signs of instability, I would be on top of it."

"So, based on your instincts, you made a willful decision to lie to me by omission?"

"Come on, Kate." The tips of Cole's ears were bright red. "We're not talking about impropriety here. I didn't think it mattered."

"You didn't think it mattered?"

"Scoot's a good cop, dammit," he said, making a valiant attempt to keep his voice down. But his eyes continued to punctuate each word. "He's racked up hundreds of collars. That doesn't make him homicidal."

"No such thing as a crooked cop?"

"Scoot's a good cop," he repeated stubbornly.

As silence stretched between them, Kate decided to let go of it for the time being. "I'm only trying to do my job, Cole."

"Be wary of hysterical accusations."

"I'm looking for accurate—"

"What is it you still don't trust, Kate? Is it me—or just my instincts?"

Kate gave him the only answer she could, and that was silence.

They'd gone less than a mile from the victim's house when Cole suddenly pulled off the road and stopped the car. He tugged at his lower lip while his eyes searched her face. She sat rigidly, as though a stiff spine would give her courage for what was to follow.

"Kate...there's something I need to say, but I don't know how."

Here it comes.

"I'm telling you this because I don't want you to think I'm callous."

Kate turned away from him, fighting tears. "Don't do this," she whispered.

He reached for her, but she recoiled.

"Kate—"

"Don't touch me," she said. *Not if it's to push me out of your life again.*

"Okay, okay. I won't," he assured her, patting the space between them with his hands. "I'm just trying to say that working together, being together again, is going to be complicated.... It's going to take some time.... Please try to understand."

"I understand perfectly," she said quietly. The beginnings of a headache bounced inside her head.

"No. I don't think you do."

"Stop it. I can figure this out for myself. I don't need you to draw me a picture."

"Dammit, I'm trying to say that it won't work—a night here, an afternoon there."

Kate's breathing stopped as she felt the old, familiar pain rising inside her. She no longer tried to conceal it. Tears spilled over her lower lashes. Her lips quivered. Just like that? He could do this to her again?

"Just *say* the words," she insisted.

He furrowed his brow while he puzzled her reaction.

"I have tickets to the Suns basketball game tonight. They're playing the Knicks. Why don't we just relax together—see where it takes us?"

Emotion tightened her throat. She turned to meet his gaze and found sincerity there. Was he telling her that he still loved her? That he wasn't going to let her go this time? All her previous resolutions to remain aloof, to act as if he didn't reside inside her heart, abandoned her. There was no time for anything but honesty this go-around.

"The last time the Suns played the Knicks," she whispered, wiping tears with one hand, "the coliseum roof nearly came down."

Kate sent him a hesitant smile. Cole laughed. They both laughed—something they had done very little of since her return.

"Right," he said finally, staring at her intently.

Sunlight changed the color of his eyes to a transparent shade of bluish gray that she found mesmerizing. She stared back for a brief moment, yearning swelling her heart. *Take it slowly,* a little voice warned her. *One small step at a time.*

"What about it?" Cole murmured.

"I'm all for the idea, but I'm not up to that level of energy tonight. Could I have a rain check?"

"In writing if you like."

Nothing more was said for a while. Then she asked softly, "What are you doing for lunch today?"

Because she'd made an effort, so did he. "How about hamburgers and fries to go?"

"What'd you have in mind?"

"How about a picnic? We're only fifteen minutes from Lake Pleasant."

She said yes, without any second thoughts.

"What do we talk about?" she asked.

"We match wits with a psychopath."

"Are you serious?"

"Dead serious."

Kate's battered spirit rose. If they were going to work this case through together, they would do it on common ground. They just needed to find it.

WITH RENEWED determination, Cole turned onto the Lake Pleasant Road. Too much was at stake to mess up now.

He parked his car atop the Waddell Dam to give Kate a bird's-eye view of the lake and surrounding area. For a while, they ate lunch in companionable silence. Kate began to sort out her thoughts aloud.

She looked out the window at the expanse of cactus-covered hills as she spoke. "He brought one of them here, didn't he?" she asked softly.

Cole had maneuvered his Caprice around to face the highway. He pulled the keys out of the ignition, but left them jingling in his hand.

"This is where he hung the first corpse."

It sounded gruesome, saying the words out loud, allowing the import of them to sink in. Kate stared at the surrounding area.

"Why here?" he asked, trying to puzzle it out.

"Exposure...easy detection," Kate said. "Have you wondered about victim access?"

"I've thought about it plenty. The implications are staggering. Scoot is running down everybody who might have come in contact with the victims twenty-four hours prior to the attack."

"Except for Phyllis Coffer, who was out on bond, the other victims were in custody until the moment the Judge cut them loose—post-hearing."

"If the court is a connection," Cole said, and it was a big if, "the immediate problem we face is whether or not to go public with the information." Kate nodded her agreement while his mind considered possible scenarios. His eyes gravitated to hers as the seed of an idea sprouted. "The trail could lead back to anyone." The possibility left him cold, sent his thoughts reeling.

"Anyone who's involved in the system," Kate began, "has access to the records, and could have been familiar with all four victims. Court dockets list addresses."

"Turning professionals inside out won't sit well with them," Cole said, turning to gauge her reaction.

"For the time being, let's keep it under wraps."

"In the interests of the investigation."

"I'd like to know who was in your dad's courtroom Friday afternoon."

"Maybe we should ask him."

Kate rested her head against the seat, and let her eyes half close. It made him feel good that she could relax around him.

"Tired?" he murmured.

"No, comfortable." But as soon as the words were out, she straightened. "I suppose in a professional capacity you're well acquainted with the employees passing through the Judge's courtroom."

"I've got a working knowledge. What types are you looking for?"

"Now who's doing psychological profiles, Chief?"

"Goes with the territory," he answered wryly. "You've got to be able to type people in my business."

A stream of traffic rolled past on its way to the lake. But Cole's attention was focused on his companion. "I'm glad you're here, Kate," he said quietly.

"Even if I was the mayor's idea?"

"One of the things the mayor wants is to look good, so he called out the feds. Another is to make me look bad. He did that when he called you, and that's okay with me. But I can't turn this investigation over to a politician, even if it means withholding information from the mayor." He watched her expression intently for a sign. "I have to know where you stand, Kate, one way or the other."

"It's not that easy," she protested.

"I'm not asking you to lie. I'm just asking you to keep the details of this case between the two of us."

"You're asking me to set aside work ethics pro bono," Kate said.

He was. And it bothered him. But nothing less would work. He'd never asked for more, or needed as much.

Kate was clearly torn. She bit at her lower lip, her eyelids closed to seal in her internal conflict.

"Kate, I'm trying to trap a killer who refuses to abide by the rules of fair play.... If the mayor's office takes over this investigation, innocent people are going to suffer...even die. I need you on my side—if you think you can keep up."

"My personal life is a separate matter. I have no choice but to cooperate with you in the investigation," she replied. "And there I'll match you stride for stride."

He had her support. It was enough for now.

THE SPIRIT OF competition welled inside Kate—and she liked it. A bit of competitiveness would give the investigation a badly needed shot in the arm. Regardless of their personal feelings, there couldn't be any rivalry between them. That kind of situation between separate agencies created gaping holes large enough for criminals to slip through.

After spending most of the day with him examining the victim's house, and making notes on an endless parade of details about the crime, she'd driven herself back to the cottage in a rental car. Now it was necessary for her to assemble a profile. She was beginning to feel well acquainted with the killer. Maybe a bit too comfortable with him.

Kate shrugged. There was something she had to attend to. She could put it off until she was driven to do it, or she could go now and politely pay the McGuires a visit. She agonized over the decision. Even though she took comfort in the McGuires, she was wary of facing an immediate inquiry about their son. If her guess was right, Cole was ushering Scoot into a basketball game right about now.

She emerged from the shower feeling cleaner but still tired. She slipped on slacks and a cotton top, tied her tennis shoes, then headed out the door to descend the terraced patios separating the cottage from the main dwelling.

The McGuires' guesthouse rested on a knoll apart from everything else. It was nothing less than a retreat. The distance between the cottage and the main house was considerable compared to city standards. The desert hills created precious privacy for those who resided in the area.

"Anyone home?" Kate called out as she passed through the kitchen door.

Her voice reverberated through the rambling, ranch-style house. The question seemed safe enough until she heard what sounded like an argument inside. She was nearly to the Arizona room, when the sound of voices sprang up like a brick wall. They stopped her cold.

"I'm only worried about you," Libby said in a voice tinged with desperation.

"That's precisely the problem," the Judge informed her in a tone Kate had never heard him use before.

It stunned her. It embarrassed her, as well. She wanted desperately to be anywhere else but here. It was the first time she'd ever heard the McGuires argue, and she didn't want them to know that she had overheard. She was taking slow but deliberate backward steps when Libby suddenly entered the kitchen. The Judge continued to rant in the other room, while Libby looked stricken.

"*Kate*... dear." She lowered her voice, but it must have been loud enough for the Judge to have heard, because a sudden silence filled the house.

"I—I'll come back—"

"Please don't leave, Kate," Libby pleaded. "Iced tea's in the refrigerator." There was a pause. "We can all use something to drink."

Kate forged a feeble smile of consent, then poured herself a glass and strode into the Arizona room behind Libby. The television was tuned to a basketball game, with the sound muted. Folded into his favorite wing chair, the Judge slouched in a most undignified manner. Fatigue shadowed his eyes.

"Hello, Your Honor," Kate said in greeting.

"Hello, Kate," he said warmly. "Long day?"

"Tedious."

"Is it safe to ask how the investigation is going?"

"Slowly, at the moment."

"Mail came for you today," Libby told her. "I left it on the kitchen table in the cottage."

"Thanks," Kate said, realizing she had failed to notice it. It felt good having Libby mother-hen her once again. She wondered if Cole realized just how fortunate he was to have such wonderful parents.

"I left your address with the office," Kate explained. "I didn't think you would mind."

"Of course not, dear," Libby assured her.

"Would you have a typewriter around I could use while I'm here?"

"Cole's old portable from college is here somewhere," Libby offered. "I'll dig it out before you leave."

"Thanks," Kate told her.

It was getting late, but there was still enough sunlight to create the illusion of melting butter oozing over everything.

"Where's Cole?" Libby asked softly.

"On his way to a basketball game," Kate replied.

"I might have known," the Judge said.

Kate continued to fill them in on the events of the day, explaining away Cole's absence. Libby was demonstrating the proper amount of disappointment, but she appeared stressed and tired, her face drawn.

"There's something I'd like to ask you, Your Honor."

Libby stiffened visibly. The Judge remained unmoved.

Kate sucked in a deep breath for courage, hating it when curiosity devoured her. "Please tell me what you think," Kate began. "If the victim wakes and provides us with a positive identification, will the lower court waive the preliminary hearing on this case?"

Libby's eyes widened, but she relaxed a tick. The Judge hesitated with his response. Of course, he would study it first. Consider it. Process possibilities. He was a fine jurist, guided by wisdom and experience.

"The justice court will do what they've been doing up until now—exactly as they please."

"Even if we secure a positive identification?"

He said nothing. Perhaps he hadn't heard the question. Every newspaper circulating in the area had detailed accounts of Friday night's attack on Phyllis Coffer. There were no pictures of the victim. And if not for Grace Van Buren zapping the forces with the Freedom of Information Act, there probably wouldn't have been a story this soon, either.

"Depends on the precinct," he said finally, smiling a little grimly.

From his monotone, Kate detected a certain cool indifference, and she wondered if her curiosity, by asserting itself, had offended him.

"With an eyewitness, the prosecuting attorney will want to sidestep the justice court and grand-jury the case," she said. "Don't you think?"

"That's one way for the prosecutor to keep his cards facedown until trial discovery. It's what I would do."

"I've never considered you pro-prosecution," she said.

"That conclusion is precisely why I'm stingy with my opinions." Then he added, "I'm not pro-prosecution."

Kate rested her tumbler of iced tea on a glass-topped Mexican pot. Reclining on the low-profile sofa, she admired the huge expanse of window allowing a view of the Hassayampa River snaking across the desert sand below. It was good to be here.

"Are you any closer to understanding this case?" the Judge asked.

She had been watching Libby sipping a vodka on the rocks. Cole's mother did not display the slightest indication of having had a drink. Her capacity for alcohol amazed Kate. Libby had switched to vodka—the no-telltale substitute—while Kate's thoughts had been far away.

"We think we have a link," Kate said, exercising care not to sound excited. "You may find this curious, but we think the judicial process might provide the key."

The Judge did not answer. Nor did his expression change. Kate had always admired his discipline. She could read nothing in his face when he started to rise. His control made him an effective jurist.

"What do you know about Nan Dupree? She's the public defender who represented Phyllis Coffer."

"Surely you don't believe she had anything to do with the victim's attack," the Judge countered.

"I haven't had a chance to meet with her yet, though I'm anxious to, since she was the last known person to talk to the victim before the assault." Kate veered off onto new ground. "We're still trying to assemble a list of any known enemies."

The Judge took a deep breath, closed his eyes, and pinched the bridge of his nose while shaking his head.

"Nan Dupree has been a friend and colleague for a long time. I'm afraid she wasn't cut out to defend. Should have been a prosecutor. Frankly, I think it was defending those guilty ones that changed her." He turned his head away. His face revealed a touch of sadness at having said that. "It's such a shame."

"Where is she?" Kate asked.

His brows knit over brooding dark eyes as he spoke. "I don't know. This sounds serious," the Judge observed, though clearly his mind was elsewhere.

Kate's headache pounded with hurricane force, a number ten. It became difficult for her to focus. She had stopped at a pharmacy on the way home and bought aspirin. She doubted that the medicine would be powerful enough to dull the throbbing pain.

"I don't suppose the victim is expected to survive such a brutal attack?" Libby asked.

Kate's stomach shuddered once before she drew herself straight and contolled it.

"It's possible," she said. "We still have hope."

The Judge's forehead wrinkled, his lips were set, his eyes were glazed in thought.

"If you have a possible eyewitness, why all the fuss over Nan Dupree?" Libby asked with a sudden intensity.

She had a good face, and most of the time her expression was warm and motherly. The strain of the murders was apparent, however. Her smile had faded, and her expression went through an odd alteration. She was suddenly gone, disengaged. Her eyes were blank, and she gave Kate a look empty of emotion.

"Just routine, but she needs to get in touch with us," Kate answered.

"I'm certain she'll do what's right," the Judge said.

"I hope the end is near," Libby said, her eyes fixed on the Judge, her expression solemn.

There was a flash in her eyes that Kate had seen in quail: wild, anxious, desperate. It was just a flicker, and then it was gone. Libby needed to take better care of herself. But all of her time was devoted to her family. The Judge. Cole. They were her world. She made certain it was a comfortable, happy one.

"We're doing our best," Kate reassured her. She bit her lip and glimpsed the big clock on the wall. It showed ten minutes after seven. The room had grown dim. The horizon had swallowed the sun. Random spears of bright light lingered in the evening sky. "I have a profile to assemble. Will you both excuse me?"

"I'll walk you to the door," Libby said.

"No, no. Stay where you are. I'll find my way out. Good night," Kate said, knowing she'd gone as far as she dared go.

Chapter Eleven

"Problems, Chief?" Scoot asked.

Cole stood at the French doors in his living room, staring out while Scoot slouched in a chair, rolling a cigarette between the fingers of his burly hand, and shredding sunflower seeds with his teeth.

"Why do you eat those damn things?" Cole snapped, ready to snarl at the first disagreeable word.

"'Cause you don't like me smoking in here. So what's got you so tight? Maybe you been reading too much of the newspaper."

"Right," Cole said, wishing he could join his old partner and friend in his nonchalance, but this press leak was eating at him. Today he had read about the *only* aspect of the case he'd held back: the connection with his father. The leak had resulted in wannabe killers calling in by the droves to pinpoint hanging locations.

"Who leaked it?" the detective asked, driving right to the point with a low, booming voice that could have carried the length of a football field.

Again, Cole considered the possibilities. A quantum leap wasn't necessary. To date, the mayor had been at the root of all of his problems. But someone had to have leaked the information to the mayor. He'd considered calling Kate, but he'd been too angry, too emotional. He'd wait until morning.

"Can we talk about something else?" Cole asked.

"The mayor makes it sound like Kate's heading things."

Cole shifted his gaze back to Scoot without comment.

"He had to throw the press a bone," Scoot grumbled. "Too bad it had to be one of yours."

"A fed should be enough to satisfy the vultures."

"The man has been staying up too late at night watching those crime movies. His statement sounded like something straight out of *Slaughter of the Lambs.*"

"The Silence of the Lambs," Cole corrected. "If you're going to quote movie titles, get them straight."

"Whatever." He pointed a cold cigarette at Cole. "The mayor has called a conference for Monday afternoon. Think about it." Scoot made a face that not even his mother would have kissed.

"Just what we need. A roomful of cops, Kate—and a politician suffering from dementia," Cole added.

Scoot had to grin. "Answer me this," he said. "What the hell is a headhunter going to add to the investigation?"

"We're going to find out."

"She handles herself well, don't she?"

"Maybe we should, too." Cole looked at the detective, ignoring the implied question.

"She's got a good head on her shoulders, too good if you ask me, but I ain't holding that against her."

"A man's gotta make certain sacrifices."

The detective smiled, pleased with himself. When his chief was chewing on him, things were as close to normal as they could get. "No point in stewing about the press leak."

"Who said I was stewing?"

"We're talking about the Judge's name being linked to a serial killer."

"Leave my father out of this, dammit. He's not involved."

Cole fought off a dizzying wave of despair. He wished the mayor could get it through his fat head that when he sabotaged his chief of police, he also sabotaged the investigation.

"I didn't say he was. But we've still got an investigation to run."

"Can we finish this discussion in the morning?"

"Correct me if I'm wrong," Scoot said, ignoring Cole's plea, "but we have us a live one in the hospital." He fixed his buddy with a wry smile. "Let the mayor say what he likes. It ain't gonna stick."

"Yeah? Well, even if you could do something about the mayor, Murphy's Law is racking up overtime." Cole knew he was deflecting his frustration—and that Scoot could handle it. Theirs was a unique relationship.

"Look," Scoot said, displaying two thick fingers toward heaven, "two ways to read this. If the victim gets tired of this Sleeping Beauty routine, we got ourselves a material witness. If she croaks, we got ourselves a bullet for ballistics."

"That's one hell of a trade-off." Cole mellowed a bit. "I think we'd better understand who this madman is if we're going to do our job."

Scoot nodded. He'd been a good street cop, a better detective.

"That's what I'm here trying to tell you," the C of D said. "Kate's just doing a job, like the rest of us." Then, in the same breath, he added, "I don't happen to think that her job has any connection with ours. But it ain't nothing personal."

Tension worked its way up the back of Cole's neck. A light breeze floated inside. March always meant chilly nights, cool enough so that you still needed a blanket on your bed.

"She bothers you," Scoot said, cutting straight through Cole's carefully erected facade of indifference. "A woman smart like that, she's bound to get inside your head."

"Who?"

Scoot rolled his eyes at Cole.

"Yes, she bothers me," Cole said abruptly.

Scoot grinned like a well-rewarded kid, stood and looked at the floor while he kneaded the back of his thick neck. Cole followed him to the door, wondering what that was all about.

KATE JOGGED TOWARD the guesthouse, taking in sunset and desert and dry heat while she indulged in a replay of Cole's lovemaking last night. They both had wanted it, so who was she going to blame it on? No full moons, no werewolves, but definitely animal instinct.

Halfway to the cottage she called it quits because her calves hurt, and walked the rest of the way.

For all her dread over the prospect of fielding questions about Cole from Libby and Judge McGuire, not once had they asked how things were between her and their son. Perhaps they thought it was none of their business, that it was just too soon to pry. Whatever their reasons, she was grateful they hadn't prodded.

She was out of breath when she reached the cottage. The telephone was ringing as she opened the door. With the receiver in her hand, she drew in a slow breath before pressing it to her ear.

"Hello?" she said while her breathing still hitched.

"Hello, Doc," came a gruff voice. "Know who this is?"

She recognized Scoot's voice. But it didn't matter. He was going to tell her, anyway.

"Detective Grasso."

"What's up, Scoot?"

On the edge of that realization, Kate also knew the cop had a juicy morsel for her to digest, or he wouldn't be calling her at home on a Sunday night. She had a hidden agenda for this conversation, too. She couldn't help but wonder who Cole had taken to the basketball game instead.

"Lab results say the guard had clean hands. He might have carried in a gun, but he didn't fire it."

Another crumb to swallow, Kate thought without replying.

"So what do you think, Doc? We got ourselves a psychopath who wears gloves?" Kate pulled in air while she waited for a break in his monologue. "If you ask me, his statement's too pat."

"It wouldn't hurt to check out everyone in Judge McGuire's court that day."

"Yeah, well, they don't record the spectators."

"I wasn't talking about spectators."

"Whose throat you grabbing for?"

"Come on, Detective."

"You read the guard's written statement?" he asked, changing directions.

She blamed her impatience on fatigue.

"I read it," she said in an even voice.

Scoot had something. He was taking his time with it.

"That was only the dress rehearsal."

"I'm not following," she said impatiently.

"I got the live performance today," he informed her in a glowing voice.

He grew quiet waiting for her reaction. The silence was unnerving, causing Kate to lose more control. But it was unlikely he would bounce his discovery off her until she showed some proper manners.

"Are we talking short-term memory loss here?" she asked.

"Yeah. You want to know how he illuminates me?"

Finally. Kate set his rhetorical question aside and began reconstructing the guard's written statement. There had been nothing illuminating about it.

"Share it, please," she said quietly.

"I pay him a little visit today, poke around on him until he suddenly remembers something important. 'An oversight,' he says. Me, I got my own thoughts on dementia."

Selective memory was enough to make anybody suspicious, but a cop more so. Playing the game, Kate repeated the question. "What did the guard tell you?"

Scoot was having a good time with his find. He knew he had Kate dangling on the edge.

"You ever heard of a reporter by the name of Grace Van Buren?"

"We've met."

"This guard, see, he gets in the elevator and rides to the fourth floor, right?"

She had no idea where he was going with this.

"That's consistent with his statement," she conceded.

"Yeah? Well, this ain't. Grace is in the lobby when the guard returns to report the attempted murder—that's how she finds out that fate's just dumped the story of the century into her lap. She rolls inside the elevator, too, rides to the fourth floor with him to check on the victim. Here's the good part. While he's consoling the maid, Gracie is shooting rolls of film."

Kate's mind jumped to a death-investigation class she had taken at Quantico, when her imagination had geared up and gone into overtime. Once again it was running rampant.

"The guard gets scared, says he puts Grace and her camera and the maid on the elevator and sends them down."

Kate heard Scoot suck deeply on his cigarette. She waited, adrenaline pumping, trying to put logic to these new revelations.

"It gets better," he drawled. "Now the guard's riding down alone when the box makes a scheduled stop on the third floor because of the renovation going on there. That's when he spots 'Simon Says.'" Another pause. She wished he would get to the obvious. "He ain't alone."

Kate gripped the receiver in both hands. She was grateful Scoot couldn't see her there, hanging on his every word, heart pounding like a rookie cop puzzling out her first case. Patience had turned on her like the Grim Reaper. And all she could do was sit by helplessly.

"Naturally, I figure Gracie has some explaining to do." Another drag on his cigarette. "And turns out Nan Dupree's with Simon."

"Grace told you that?"

"She never returned my call. Simon LaRoush did, though. He's on his way down from the fourth floor where he's been to see Judge McGuire. Says he uses the stairs because renovation has maligned the elevators." He sucked on his cigarette. "It's a real mess."

Kate was making notes and getting edgy, and he seemed to know that. So far, all he'd told her about was a prosecuting attorney spotted with a defense attorney, and an overzealous reporter dirtying a crime scene.

"Simon finds her on the third floor, having herself a little cry over something Judge McGuire has said to her. Simon comforts her."

"And the guard spots them," Kate said. "Did you talk to Nan Dupree?"

"Nope. But there's more. Simon says he never gets to talk to the Judge because there's already someone in chambers with him."

"Seems everybody had appointments with Judge McGuire Friday evening."

"That ain't all," Scoot added quickly.

She should have known he'd hold back a wild card for the grand finale.

"Simon says he hears—and get this—" Scoot broke off abruptly to indulge a dramatic pause. Kate was too startled to object. Her pulse raced as she processed the possibilities.

"Simon says he hears a woman's voice coming from the Judge's chamber. Mad as hell, this woman is."

"Nan Dupree?"

"Simon don't know."

"You want to tell me what the conversation was about?"

"Don't know that, either," he said flatly. "A lot of 'back and forth' going on."

Kate hadn't expected this, and preferred moving slowly with the implications.

"He doesn't see who it is and he fails to recognize the voice. How can he be certain of anything?"

"The woman's crying, see. Simon thinks he's about to walk in on something he shouldn't. Something personal, maybe. Says he just turned around and walked to the stairwell in the outside foyer.

"You ain't gonna like this, but, word has it these two are having an affair."

"Nan Dupree and Simon?"

"I was talking about Nan Dupree and Judge McGuire."

For a moment Kate felt too stunned to think.

"Bad news travels fast," Scoot said disgustedly. "It's become an item lately."

It occurred to her that he could be right. It also occurred to her to thank him. But finally, she just gave up the notion of courtesy.

"When can I expect to have a copy of the department's report on the Phyllis Coffer attack?" she asked instead.

She hoped the note of kindness in her voice would suffice to convey her gratitude to Scoot for his consideration.

"I can drive it up tonight."

"Tomorrow morning is soon enough. I'll be in town then."

"Don't let all of this get you down."

"Right."

"Get some rest," he said bluntly. "You sound ragged as hell. Don't worry, you'll be hearing from me if anything turns a different shade."

"Okay."

"Got a pencil?" he asked. "You can take down my beeper number."

"Do you think that's necessary?"

A string of numbers was his answer. "You need me, you beep me," he said.

"Thank you. I'll try not to abuse the privilege."

"Hey?" he asked. "You still on the line?"

"I'm still here."

"Remember the bloodstains on the victim's clothes?"

Kate sat hard on the verge of exasperation, and moved to lead him forward as gently as she could.

"What about the bloodstains?"

"They're consistent with Phyllis Coffer's blood."

The victim's blood, Kate thought dismally. *It doesn't mean a thing.* The disappointment left her gasping.

"Oh, and this, too. The pathologist said the condition of the victim's hands indicated Coffer had given back some of what she got. The knuckles were torn and scabbed black with dried blood. Someone else's blood."

He'd saved the best for last, and it carried the force of an atom bomb. She digested the information to put it with what she already knew. Had the detective failed to look for defense wounds on the victim? To cover up his oversight, had he told her there were none when she'd asked him about them at the hospital?

"Chief says hello."

"Does he know about any of this?" she asked.

"Not unless he's clairvoyant."

"It might be a good idea to brief him."

"You worry about him, do you?"

The temptation was more than she could bear. In her most professional voice she said, "We're a team."

But Scoot didn't hear those last words. He had wisely hung up.

KATE TOOK ANOTHER sip of wine, and stepped into the hot bath, a comfort always soothing to her soul. For the time being, she would allow her mind to be still. But doing so made her vulnerable, because she couldn't keep Cole's image from rushing in and shaking her up.

Maybe, she thought with surprise, her life needed shaking up. And to that end, a compulsive psychopath was doing a fine job all by himself.

Except for the light from the candles she had lit, the cottage was completely dark. She eased into the warm water until it lapped at her chin. The guesthouse had been so still that each time it groaned or creaked, she'd jumped visibly.

Kate had been entertaining a solid case of nerves, but the hot water was finally smoothing out the kinks. She felt drowsy when she finally stepped out of the tub. After towel-drying, she slipped into a cotton sleep shirt and padded into the kitchen to replenish her wineglass.

She'd left the bottle open on the kitchen table to breathe. When she reached for it, she noticed the piece of mail with her name and the McGuires' address on it. The San Domingo postmark puzzled her. She opened it with a kitchen knife and, inside, found a note folded in half. It was a typed message.

The print squirmed before Kate's eyes. She was so engrossed, so stung, her eyes refused to blink. They were burning, tearing, as she leaned close to read the message.

I'll be watching you....
Don't let them contaminate the land.

The stony silence in the room screamed back at her now. She took a deep breath, studying the words. A killer with an aversion to dirt? Infection? Her overwhelming desire to know him escalated. She wanted to know what had created the psychopath in him. She already knew what nurtured it.

Kate returned the page to its envelope, noting how steady her hands appeared, even though she felt drained physically. She put both articles into a plastic bag, and was on the point of calling Cole and telling him about the note, but something stopped her. She didn't want to discuss this with anyone until she'd had time to digest it.

She carried her wine into the bedroom. The king-size bed was inviting. She drained her glass, then crawled between the sheets. Not until she had the spread pulled up to her neck, did she let out a sigh of relief. The wine finally kicked in, and she began to relax. She snuggled into the down pillows, growing drowsy.

She hadn't been aware of falling asleep. Now she sat bolt upright in bed, rivulets of cold sweat soaking the sheets twisted around her. When her eyelids flew open, she was certain that someone had been standing over her. Her heart slammed violently against her rib cage and her breath was coming in short gasps. Confused, she called out the first name that came to mind.

"Cole?"

No one answered.

A dream. It was only a dream she'd been having. *So sleepy,* Kate thought. Her eyelids refused to stay open. When she opened them again, she had no idea how much time had elapsed, and at first she thought the pounding on the front door was part of a nightmare.

The pounding persisted. She wasn't certain it was any more real than the eyes she'd imagined staring down at her. But when the noise continued, she crawled out of bed to investigate.

It was nine-thirty. She'd been asleep for two hours. The inside temperature was sixty degrees, and she was freezing. She padded into the living room, where only moonlight illuminated the area. The entire cottage was creaking from the cold. On the way to the front door, she pulled an afghan from the sofa and wrapped it around her shoulders.

"Who's there?" she called out.

"Detective Grasso."

Scoot? Kate felt a vague sense of unease at his sudden appearance, so soon after she'd believed someone had entered the cottage. Then she shrugged it aside and unlocked the door and pulled it open.

"What's wrong?" she asked.

"Not a damn thing if you'd find a place to stay closer to town." He breezed past her and slapped a legal-size brown envelope down on the coffee table. "Thought you might like to read my report."

His unannounced visit didn't speak for his intelligence, but he was a get-the-job-done sort of guy.

"Right this minute?"

"Uh-huh."

"You drove to Wickenburg to hand-deliver your police report?" she asked.

"Mind if I turn on some lights?"

"Why not make yourself at home?"

The smile was broad and generous, and the eyes friendly. It was hard to be angry at him. At least he wasn't asking her anything about Cole. Not that she would have answered.

He headed for the kitchen, where he set about making coffee. She paused, her eyes scanning the brown envelope. *Any more bombs?* she silently wondered.

"Looks like you been working," he muttered, letting his fingers tap-dance across the typewriter keyboard.

"Oh," Kate mumbled to herself. Libby must have brought the typewriter up while she was sleeping.

"You got a tape recorder around?" Scoot asked while he searched the cabinet for coffee.

He smelled of cigarettes and cheap mouthwash.

"No," she said distractedly. "Coffee's in the refrigerator."

The square face bore strain, and it was no wonder. When did this man sleep?

"I thought we might give the tape an ear," he mumbled, plucking the coffee can from the refrigerator door.

"The *tape?*" Kate echoed, still numbed from sleep, or lack of it.

She was beginning to form a different opinion of Cole's C of D. He wasn't slow, or thick between the ears. He paced himself. And he was tenacious.

"The one you lifted from Coffer's." He moved his bulky frame around with the ease of a ballet dancer. "You doctor yours?" he asked, pointing to a small bottle of what appeared to be bourbon at her.

"No."

"Suit yourself," he said, loading the tray with mugs and coffeepot and the bottle of liquor. "I brought a recorder," he said. "Mind if I smoke?"

"Open the patio doors, please."

He nodded and extracted a cigarette from his breast pocket. Once the doors were ajar, he lit the cigarette and inhaled deeply.

"Where is it?" he asked.

She knew he was talking about the tape, and she told him she would get it. It was nearly ten o'clock now and she was about to waste the better part of another hour with Scoot, playing a tape that might or might not harbor something worth hearing. The profile had to be completed before Tuesday morning. What was she thinking? She hadn't traveled halfway across the United States to humor a burned-out detective.

"Can't find it?" he asked, watching her empty the contents of her bag.

"It's here," she said defensively.

"You sure you put it there?"

"Positive."

Why was she defending herself to Scoot? He'd dropped in unannounced. She was the one who should have been short on goodwill.

"Want me to help you look?"

She stared him into silence, more determined than ever to produce the tape. But the possibility was diminishing by the minute as she eliminated each place it could have been.

"Maybe I should come back another time," Scoot conceded—finally.

Kate squeezed her eyes shut and stiffened for a brief moment.

"I have a profile to prepare," she said quietly.

Scoot fished inside his pants pocket for his keys, ready to honor her unspoken request.

"You shoulda said so," he grumbled, pointing a cigarette at her and using it to tap out the syllables of his words as he spoke to her.

There was no smile. He wasn't being funny anymore. He was aware that the most difficult, time-consuming part of any investigation was profiling the killer.

"I'll leave the recorder," he offered. "When the tape shows up, you can listen to it."

She didn't answer him. At that moment she really didn't feel up to listening to the tape or to him. She was tired. And sore. And she was irritable.

"Thanks for bringing the report," she said, making a feeble stab at courtesy. "I know you had better things to do on a Sunday night."

"I'm outta here," he told her. "Keep your doors locked."

She let the remark go. But the minute he was outside and driving away, she secured the flimsy locks and pulled the drapes before clearing the coffee table. The sound of glass hitting glass echoed shrilly in the empty room.

She wouldn't look at Scoot's police report tonight, or hunt for the tape, she told herself as she shrugged off her robe. Tonight she would pamper herself, forget about the case, forget about the tape. She would forget about the victim lying in a hospital bed, she would forget about the murders of three human beings. And she would forget about the killer.

Cole McGuire, however, was another matter entirely....

Chapter Twelve

A lot could be gleaned from the tone of a voice.

Kate arrived at her office at San Domingo police headquarters before eight to find Cole resting comfortably behind her desk.

"You after a head start?" Kate asked.

"Uh-huh."

Kate knew she faced a confrontation.

"What's on your mind, Chief?"

"Sit down," Cole said flatly.

"Sounds serious."

"Coffee?"

Kate shook her head, growing impatient. "Why don't you say what you have to say and let me get to work?"

"The paper goes better with coffee," he said, slapping the folded wad down in front of her. "What made you do it, Kate? Is this why you came back? To hurt me the way I—"

"Not another word, damn you."

He stood then, jamming his hands into his pockets, balling them into fists. He paced briefly. Then he picked up the paper and read from it: "'The mayor's office confirmed yesterday that the FBI agent assigned to the Hangman homicides has uncovered a piece of the puzzle surrounding the case. The connection linking the victims lies within their court adjudications....'"

"You're accusing me of leaking this to the press?" she demanded.

"No," he said, his tone of voice exaggerated from control. "I'm asking why. How could you knowingly drag my family into this?"

"I gave you my word that I would keep this information under wraps—"

"You set me up for this, didn't you? You wanted to get even—"

"Stop it, dammit!"

"Or was this about personal glory?"

Kate stood, ramrod straight, ready to go toe-to-toe with Cole.

"Who the hell do you think you are—tossing out accusations like this about me? Did it ever occur to you that *I* didn't leak this to the press?"

But she *had* confided in the mayor with the information. He'd been the first person she'd encountered after making the discovery, and unwisely or not, she'd been emotional enough to blurt the finding to him. But she'd emphasized the confidentiality. Either way she went with this little gem, Cole would have his answer.

"Why'd you come back, Kate?"

"Did it ever occur to you that I didn't want to take this case in the first place?"

"Then why did you?"

"I was persuaded to believe I could help. I still believe that. Otherwise, I'd be on the first plane out of here heading east."

"You've destroyed two lives with this." Kate looked away in an attempt to block the pain his words carried. "Do you know how that feels?"

She whirled back again, eyes dark and impassioned. "You're damned right I do." Her breath caught as she struggled to regain control.

"Kate, I'm—"

"What is it about me that makes you so bitter? Let me tell you what I think. You're redirecting your own guilt at me, dammit. Because you're the one who really checked out eighteen months ago. That's right, Cole. You were afraid to commit." Tears were dangerously close. "I'm getting off this treadmill."

"Wait—"

"To hell with you!"

There was no point in hanging around. Kate knew what a bout of temper did to her. As soon as she'd pushed through the back door, she broke into a run. Once inside her car, she headed straight for the freeway, without any destination in mind, just as long as it was away from Cole McGuire.

IT WAS NEARLY nine-thirty that night when Kate turned onto the ranch road leading to the cottage. She'd driven to Flagstaff and back to unwind. Damn the mayor. Damn the investigation. And damn Cole McGuire.

She glanced at the McGuires' house. These murders had taken their toll on everyone. Libby was obviously an emotional wreck, and the added stress had brought on her sleepwalking. Since Kate had arrived, she had seen every light in the house burning each night. Not tonight, though.

An uneasy feeling squeezed Kate when she found the cottage door open. She felt certain she had locked it, but tonight she had been questioning everything. She stepped inside, secured the lock, then dropped her bag on the kitchen table.

She busied herself in the kitchen, because work always served her best when she was in distress. Soon the aroma of freshly brewed coffee drifted through the house. But the pain inflicted by Cole's words persisted. She collapsed into one of the kitchen chairs and covered her face with her hands. She began to sob softly, tears breaking to roll down her cheeks. With a growing sense of futility filling her, Kate wept until she had cried her heart out.

Why had she accepted this assignment? Why had she thought she could help? A relationship with Cole simply wasn't meant to be. Professional *or* personal. No amount of hoping or wishing was going to resurrect it. She was reaching for a napkin to wipe her eyes when she noticed the piece of mail on the kitchen table. That would explain the open door. One of the McGuires had delivered it.

After she had opened the envelope and unfolded the note, she stared blindly at the printed message as bile crept up her throat and her heart thudded against her ribs. She mouthed the written words on it.

I'm still watching you. I've left you a present. In the bedroom. Under your pillow.

Kate felt a viselike pressure rapidly forcing the air from her lungs while her eyes darted around the room in search of anything that moved. Her fear was so real it was like another presence in the cottage.

He had been inside her bedroom. She envisioned him under the bed, right now, waiting to grab her foot when she checked her pillow. She hugged herself to stop the involuntary shivering. The dreadful flat feeling settled over her—the feeling she sometimes experienced when she viewed an especially gruesome crime scene.

Kate recovered sufficiently to stand and draw her revolver. The bedroom was just off the kitchen. Her heart pounded as she moved across the pitch-black room toward the bed. When she bumped into the night table, she felt for the lamp, then curled her fingers around the switch, heart hammering as she rotated it.

Blinding light, glaring and intrusive, illuminated the room, revealing her own reflection in the mirror. She blinked, adjusting her eyes, focusing on the pillow. Completely unnerved again, she stood frozen, weapon held high, fright distorting her features, ice running through her veins.

He'd gotten inside her house. Lift the pillow! Now!

One sweeping motion ripped back bedcovers and pillows. No bombs exploded. No monsters came. Kate ran to the bathroom to empty her stomach.

Some of the fear went away. She placed her weapon on the toilet tank, then splashed cold water on her face. She splayed her hands over her eyes. He was here with her, right now, entrenched inside her head. She reached for a towel and patted her face dry. Sucking in air for courage failed to help. She returned to the bed.

The rope remained coiled in place where her pillow had been. Kate picked it up.

She checked every room in the cottage—in the closets, under the bed. After retrieving her weapon from the bathroom, she traced her steps again. She stood inside the darkened living room of the guesthouse, staring out at the shadows and shapes of the night. Telling the McGuires about the notes was out of the question, so how could she explain a late-night intrusion? She could ask for messages, calls. Her gun would alarm them. She laid it down. But she continued to clutch the rope.

She wondered how difficult it would be for him to hide out there and grab her once she stepped outside. Snatched. Right outside her door. It happened in the city all the time. The prevailing wind was out of the southwest; the McGuires wouldn't even hear her screams.

She pulled herself together as much as she was able and unlocked the door. Peering through the crack, she considered the darkness again. She saw nothing. Heard nothing. Nothing seemed out of the ordinary. Maybe he'd encountered the McGuires and had—

"Stop it!" she said firmly.

The sound of her voice momentarily grounded her. She took a deep breath, still feeling paranoid, then slipped outside. A bat whizzed past her, generating enough fear inside her to reduce her to ooze. She slammed the front door so hard the windows vibrated. But they could have shattered and it wouldn't have stopped her. She was running for her life.

Moments later, Kate was standing in the darkened entryway to the McGuires' home. The door was unlocked, but there were no lights burning, and no one answered her calls. Enough moonlight filtered inside for her to determine that what she could see of the house had been turned upside down. She stood rooted to the floor inside the kitchen. Paralyzing fear constricted her throat until she was gasping for air. When the refrigerator came on, she cried out. Images whirled through her mind. The gruesome crime scenes. The bodies. The laughing faces at the briefing. The—*Stop!*

The telephone continued to ring long after she stopped screaming. Her spine stiffened, and her hands trembled as they smoothed back her hair. She moved in slow motion. Why answer it? It was probably *him*. Kate picked up on the fourth ring.

"Who is this?" she demanded.

"Kate?"

The second she heard Cole's voice on the other end of the telephone line, she went limp. "Oh..." came from somewhere deep inside her.

"I've been trying to reach you," he continued.

"Cole—"

She broke off, distraught, and covered the speaker portion of the receiver with her hand as tears spilled freely from her eyes.

"I've been trying to call you ever since you left here."

Kate's heart slammed against her rib cage.

"Are you all right?"

"Yes," she managed after a quick recovery. Damned if she would allow him the benefit of breaking her down.

"I'm sorry about this morning."

The need to talk to him just now was chipping away at her icy resolve, and the warmth of his voice, melted it completely. She was confused and more miserable than she'd ever been in her life.

"Cole, listen to me. Something's wrong here," she said, trying to keep her voice steady while she redirected their exchange away from the personal level.

She felt like a wild animal, frightened and in danger, with nowhere to bolt.

"What is it? Are you all right?"

"There's been an intruder. Please come—come now!" Kate's hands trembled so violently, she could barely hold on to the telephone receiver.

"Where's Mom and Dad?"

"Gone."

"Where's your weapon?"

"In the cottage."

Blood pounded in her veins as she considered the fact that someone had been inside the guesthouse. And might *still* be inside.

"Don't go back outside. Lock yourself inside the master bedroom. I'm using my mobile phone and I'm nearly there. The Judge keeps a revolver in the fireplace cleanout—"

"Hurry, Cole."

"Get the gun, Kate!"

She ran to the bedroom, switched on the light, went directly to the fireplace. Relief was short-lived.

She picked up the extension phone. "The gun isn't there."

"Look again!"

"It's gone, Cole."

First the tape, now the gun. Dread was consuming her.

"I'll dispatch a unit in the area—"

"Please, don't."

Kate knew what it meant to dispatch a patrol unit. Every available car within shouting distance would respond. If a federal agent was overreacting, it might serve to reenforce law enforcement's mistrust of the business of drawing psychological profiles.

"Hurry, Cole. I need you."

COLE ENTERED the house with his weapon drawn—and Kate's words playing over and over in his head.

Kate stood frozen, watching, waiting. His breath caught when he spotted her. He holstered his gun before he crossed the room in two strides.

"I'm all right, I'm all right," she said over and over as he crushed her against him.

"You scared the hell out of me," he murmured, pulling her next to him and stroking her head.

She looked vulnerable, like a frightened child, eyes wide, face pale.

"I scared myself," she said, pulling away.

"No sign of anyone outside. Where are my parents?"

"I found the house like this—wide open, dark and empty."

"Did my folks leave a note?"

From Kate's expression, he knew it was going to be bad.

"There's a note—" she sucked in air for courage "—from *him.*"

Cole pressed his lips together, trying to maintain self-control. "Him?"

"The killer."

"How do you know that?" He gripped her savagely by the shoulders. "Tell me now!"

"He left this for me, too."

Kate pointed the rope at him. For a moment Cole didn't respond. He couldn't. Colliding emotions squeezed him until he was struggling for breath. His heartbeat was pounding in his throat.

"Where did you get this?"

"From him."

"You saw him?" Concern reduced his voice to a hoarse whisper. "Did he hurt you?"

Kate shook her head, close to breaking down. "I didn't see him. He left it for me." Her breath caught on a sob. "He was inside my house."

"You could have interrupted him. Come here," he said, pressing the length of her against him. She pulled away slightly to look up at him. Her cheeks blanched, her eyes grew unfocused. "You're shaking. Let me get you a drink."

He felt her fingers dig into his shirt as he tried to draw back.

"It's okay," he murmured.

"Cole, I have to tell you something."

The thought increased the tension already gripping his neck.

"First you need a drink."

He went to the bar and returned with two small snifters of brandy. Kate sipped, but he gulped. It burned going down, but it warmed his insides. He needed to relax in order to sort out what had happened. He poured himself another before he felt any degree of relief. He didn't want Kate to witness him shaking like a scared rabbit. She was eyeing him curiously.

"He doesn't want to hurt me, Cole."

"That's what you had to tell me?"

"No.... This is the second communication I've had from him."

"Kate!" Frustration drove him straight to anger. "You could have told me. Why didn't you?"

"I wasn't certain. I didn't want you to think I was reactionary." She implored him with her eyes, and he relented. "I don't think he wants to hurt me."

"Dammit, Kate, use some of that profiling expertise that you're so proud of to face facts. This one is not into idle threats."

"He needs me—in a way I can't make you understand."

"Do you hear yourself?"

"It's not uncommon for psychopaths to hook up emotionally with investigators—or to send them trophies."

"You really believe that crap, don't you?"

She stiffened. "Certainly, you don't. You've made that clear already."

"This scares the hell out of me, Kate. If you were wise, you'd be frightened, too. It might keep you in touch with reality."

"People are always afraid of what they don't understand."

Something inside him clutched at his gut, but he ignored it.

"You asked me to come, Kate."

"That's right," she said calmly. "I *was* scared as hell. But if you're wanting me to cave in and be a proper lady—I can't."

"Why don't you start from the beginning?" he said softly. "Tell me what happened."

Kate nodded without lifting her gaze from the floor. She took a seat at the breakfast bar. Cole slid onto one next to her. What she told him shook him to the bone.

"I still don't understand why you didn't tell me."

She was studying the brandy glass intently. After a pause, she replied, "I didn't see any point in telling you. All it would have done was worry you, and it was my impression that there was no immediate danger."

"No immediate danger?" He looked incredulously at her. "He's killed three—a fourth is nearly dead." He raised both hands and shrugged. "I need honesty from you, Kate."

"I always tell the truth."

"No, you don't *always.* You hold back—" He decided to change directions "Isn't it possible," he began, "that he could decide to take you out, too?"

"I suppose anything is possible with a psychopath."

"You *suppose?* I want twenty-four-hour protection for you. I'll put a wire on your phone and shadows on you until he's caught."

"No. He's been watching me," Kate said, "so I should continue with my same routine. If I look accessible, we might draw him out."

Cole barely heard the words before he turned his angry impatience on her. "That won't work for me."

"That doesn't matter as long as it works for him."

"Since when do we use live bait?"

"I'm a cop, too," she whispered. "Remember?"

He remembered. That's what had him worried. He started to touch her, then hesitated.

"I want to explain about the leak," she said.

"You talk too much, you know that?" He gathered her into his arms. "Scoot already told me."

It was harder, he realized, incredibly harder to protect someone who really mattered.

COLE SEEMED SO DAMNED untouchable, was acting so detached. He had reported the break-in, and a search of both the main house and the cottage had turned up nothing. The lab people had dusted for prints. Only their mess remained. Time stood on the plus side of midnight. Tomorrow she would tidy up. Right now a pounding headache was threatening to split her head wide open. She massaged her throbbing temples.

Moments later, when Cole strode into the kitchen of the guesthouse and touched her arm, she nearly jumped out of her skin. She'd had her back to him while she peered outside. He had returned with a glass of water and a couple of aspirin. She could see he was not as detached as she'd previously thought.

"Thanks," she mumbled.

She downed them and handed him the empty glass, then curled up on the sofa. Cole followed. He flipped the empty glass upside down and began stroking it the way a gypsy might caress her crystal ball.

"I'm worried," he murmured.

"Try and relax."

She studied his expression and the unfamiliar pallor of his face.

"I don't understand this," he said. "And I don't like things I don't understand."

"It's my job to understand him."

"No mumbo-jumbo psychology is going to make me any less concerned." His jaw was flexing. "Kate,

I want to put cover on you. Now, don't say anything yet. Scoot is the only one I would trust—he could set it up—he's the best."

"And that's why you need him involved in the investigation." She went to the refrigerator and pulled out two bottles of beer. "You're making a liability out of me, Cole."

"The killer's doing that. Please, listen to me. You're the one who said he could be someone on the inside—someone with names, addresses."

"You keep forgetting that I'm a cop, too," she insisted, pointing the bottle of beer at him.

He reached for Kate's free hand, turned it palm side up, kissed it deep in its hollow. She felt a sudden rush of adrenaline with no place to go, and she drew her hand away.

"I can handle this," she insisted. "But you've got to give me a chance to do my job."

"He knows where you live, Kate. Think about it."

"He doesn't want me dead. I'm part of the challenge."

"Hell, Kate, I'm not gambling with your life. You're playing head games with a madman. Maybe you haven't realized it yet, but someone is stalking you—someone who gets off on murdering people."

"Kind of gives you the creeps, doesn't it? I don't think it's any fun for him unless he can challenge me."

"That's not what he's after, Kate. You know that."

"He wants understanding from me. That's all."

"How can you make this sound so damned simple? Play with his head after he's locked up."

"Trouble is," she said calmly, "if I don't get inside his head now and figure out what's going on there, we might never see him locked away."

"He'll screw up," Cole predicted. "And when he does, I'll be there waiting to nail him."

"He's going to strike again, and soon," Kate said. "He's in a lot of pain."

"I get the feeling you'd like to open his head and make him all better." He studied her intently, determined to understand her inexplicable interest in the madman. "You can't have it both ways. You can't be the doctor if you're going to be the cop."

"I only wish I could," she told him. Kate realized that her personal interest in a serial killer annoyed him; she also knew there was no way to make him understand it.

"He'll be glad to know he's in good hands," he said, shaking his head. "Don't get too comfortable with this thing—or you'll get hurt."

"I'm not so sure now that he wants to harm me. He's made me part of the fantasy." She slipped her arms around him, willing to take another desperate chance. She might not fear being hurt by the killer—but she had no such confidence when it came to the man standing in front of her. "Anyway, I'm receiving the very best in police protection."

"Is that right?" Cole asked in a husky voice.

"Yeah," she murmured seductively. "I'm sleeping with a cop, and I've got my own fantasy working."

He took hold of her by her shoulders. "Kate, I want you to take this seriously."

"Is DNA testing on the blood samples from the scene serious enough?" she asked. "It will take more time, but we'll get a genetic picture then."

He shook his head in frustration. She could be stubborn. Then he released her, wheeled around and walked toward the front door.

"Where are you going?" she asked.

"To get my overnight bag from the car."

"Police protection?" She was standing dangerously close.

"Lots of it."

"Round-the-clock?"

"This could get complicated."

"I've always thrived on complications."

Chapter Thirteen

Wickenburg was at its most splendid in the spring, Kate thought, admiring the brilliant orange carpet of African daisies along the river. The view from the patio at The Willows Restaurant was breathtaking. Kate could hear the Hassayampa River running. The perfect setting, with the man she loved.

She sank back in her chair. Love? Did it really come as a surprise to her—after last night, when she had expressed it physically to Cole? But what good did it do her to realize her love for him, when it only summoned up more emotions she couldn't handle? Where was all this leading? To another devastating rejection?

"What's the matter?" Cole asked from across the table.

"Nothing, just tired."

"Was breakfast in town a bad idea?"

"No, it's peaceful here."

"The fresh air should be giving you an appetite."

It was still early morning with plenty of time to drive down to San Domingo for the one o'clock presentation. A light breeze filled her with Cole's scent. Soapy, woodsy and wonderful. She smiled at him and relaxed.

"Here," she said, passing the Spanish salsa. "Indulge yourself. Makes the eggs taste better."

Cole smiled back as Kate lifted the bowl of spicy, homemade relish.

"Thanks," he said, "but if you're trying to sweat the notion of police surveillance out of me—forget it."

"There's plenty of time for that."

They exchanged a knowing glance, and Kate discovered she was no longer uncomfortable, no longer waiting to be backed into a corner. Exhilarated after a long night of lovemaking, she pushed her coffee aside.

"Did you reach Nan Dupree?" Kate asked.

"I think she's hiding."

"I don't understand."

"She's a good defense attorney, but a fragile person. She won't attend the presentation today. Her loyalty to her client makes her predictable in that regard."

Kate drew a deep breath, then exhaled a frustrated sigh. She glanced at the morning newspaper Cole was reading. "The Hangman again?"

"The press loves this guy."

"I don't think it's a good idea to allow reporters to be present at the profile today," she said.

Notoriety wasn't her style. It didn't fit into her work. All the gruesome details of this case would come out soon enough.

"I couldn't agree more."

"No press?" Kate said, arching an eyebrow.

"No press. Now let's get out of here."

"WHAT'S GRACE VAN BUREN doing here?" Kate asked Cole from the lobby of the old Orpheus Theater.

Uniforms and plainclothesmen milled about, exchanging information, smoking, sipping coffee.

Kate focused hard on him now, a steely spark in her eyes. He'd just spent the night with this woman. Protecting her. Worrying over her. He'd experienced firsthand her femininity; he knew intimately her softness, even the degree of her shyness; but this tough core, this self-possession—they were something new in her. Now it was back to murder and politics and the press.

"You're not jumping to any conclusions, are you?"

"Whoa, Chief. I've already got a question on the floor."

"You don't think I had anything to do with this?"

"No," Kate admitted. "I don't. But this isn't about what I believe. Not yet, anyway. I've asked you a question and I'd like an answer. Please."

Even in a wheelchair, the reporter was a force to contend with in a lobby filled with uniforms.

"Grace is where the news is," he said honestly.

"We had an agreement regarding the press," she reminded him. It carried the right bite. "Just ask her to leave."

"If the mayor's office informed her of the meeting, I can't do that."

"Yes, you can," Kate argued. "I've seen it done a thousand times."

"Not with this reporter, you haven't."

Cole was calm, unperturbed. He wasn't easily bullied, and he was comfortable with his decision.

Kate stood rigid, struggling not to let the importance of her plea register on her features.

"What I have to say is not for any reporter's ears. My profile could sway the direction of the investigation."

"I don't want her here, either, but it's too late to try and get rid of her. Stonewalling shoots up a red flag," Cole insisted. "I know this woman. She's as tenacious as a bulldog. And she's well versed on the Freedom of Information Act."

"So am I," Kate said, her voice cool and unruffled.

"It's my decision." His rigid tone spoke volumes.

"Thank you, Chief," she said with supreme control, "for that piece of information. I was under the impression that I might be able to contribute something to this investigation."

"Let it go, Kate. We'll discuss it later."

"Let's not discuss it at all."

She strode down the aisle toward the podium.

"Kate, wait a minute." When he caught up with her, he spoke softly into her ear. "I didn't cross the line. We're on the same side."

"Not anymore."

"I JUST MOVED the line," she told him, then headed toward the front of the theater as if she were sublimely unconcerned about Grace Van Buren or Cole McGuire. Kate assumed her place onstage while Cole approached the podium to make the introductions.

"You want to settle down in the back, there?"

Cole's deep voice projected forcefully across the aisles of seats filled to capacity. Kate had been to the Orpheus as a child. Now it appeared just as grand after restoration, but on a smaller scale. She felt a fluttering in her stomach.

All eyes were on her as she sat onstage, waiting to tell half the law enforcement of Mesquite County how to do their jobs.

The hush fell gradually, but in the end Cole had their total attention.

"I know a lot of you are working your days off or pulling a double shift, and I want to thank you." Cole paused and scanned the faces in the audience. "We need to catch this son of a bitch. And the feds have sent to us an expert in behavioral science. I expect you to show her every courtesy, but I also expect you to be the ones to bring this psycho in. Special Agent Quin is going to brief you on what makes this one tick."

Kate had prepared a short opening speech, but now she changed her mind. She cleared her throat and walked to the podium. She'd get right to the point.

"My profile draws a portrait of a madman," she began, "a psychopath who is 'guilty' as hell according to the appropriate Arizona Revised Statutes, but who is truly innocent as his problem is defined in the mental-health textbooks."

At the sound of the rear doors of the room opening, the audience began to turn to view the latecomer.

Kate brushed her ruffled bangs away from her forehead and looked toward the back of the room.

Grace Van Buren's powerful arms easily controlled the speed of her chair as she rolled herself into a better hearing position. Sometimes action spoke louder than words. But Kate already knew the extent of Grace's determination. The fact that she had broken the story about Judge McGuire's connection to the victims was still a bitter pill for Kate to swallow—even if the mayor had been the one to divulge the information to Grace.

TO COLE IT SEEMED AN eternity before Kate resumed speaking. He walked toward the rear doors to the lobby, eyes glancing at the rows of seats. He spotted his burly chief of detectives standing an aisle over by the lobby door, sandwiched between a uniformed officer and Simon LaRoush.

Conspicuously absent was the esteemed mayor of San Domingo. Trust Mayor Madden to light a fire under the men—and then to leave Kate alone to control the flames.

Straight ahead, Grace Van Buren was parked and waiting for him, halfway down from the other exit door.

"Don't think you can ply me with that silver tongue of yours," Cole warned her.

"All right. Let's cease with the small talk. We're after the same thing, Chief. Do yourself a favor, let me stay."

Cole disliked being second-guessed. But he choked it down. "Why the interest when this is just a briefing?"

"I have a fascination with federal investigators."

"Come on, Grace. I'm just doing my job—and I have to ask you to leave. No press invited."

"'Walk softly and carry a big stick'—who said that?" she asked. "My 'big stick' is the Freedom of Information Act. Don't force me to use it."

Grace's large eyes grew bigger and more determined. Cole's hope of barring the press from the profile suddenly grew slimmer.

"You're playing hardball, Grace."

"You're not exactly helpless. What's it going to be, Chief?"

Cole eyed her with raised eyebrows. "We'll listen from the lobby door."

"That works for me."

She wheeled her chair around and parked while Kate watched. Cole braced himself for a moment, waiting for Kate's fury to unleash itself. But it did not.

Whatever she was feeling, her neutral tone belied it as she continued her profile.

"The FBI's behavioral-science unit draws detailed portraits of killers by focusing on how they commit their crimes," she said calmly, glancing around the room.

With Grace at his side, Cole listened from the rear of the old theater. The stage dwarfed Kate. A four-foot podium made it even more difficult to see her delicate features, but the professional barrier added credence to her position as a federal agent.

"If you've viewed the various thrillers about psychopathic killers," Kate said, "you probably have the wrong idea about what goes on at the FBI Academy in Quantico, Virginia. Watching the behavioral-science unit actually at work is a far cry from seeing it depicted on the screen. In the real world, behavioral-science agents remain largely deskbound, in a windowless converted bomb shelter some sixty feet below ground."

Cole was impressed by Kate's ability to speak in a concise and organized fashion. He listened intently, as did his men. They were impatient, tired cops, Cole realized. He had twenty detectives assigned to the case, from every division, including Narcotics.

"Many investigators fail to distinguish between two basic types of murderers," she explained. "The organized killer and the unorganized. Our man is premeditated, intentional, and rational about his crimes."

"Speak into the mike," a uniformed officer called from a dozen rows of seats away.

Undaunted, Kate resumed her presentation. "Serial homicide involves the murders of separate victims with time breaks between crimes, as minimal as two days, to as long as weeks or months. These time breaks serve as 'cooling-off' periods."

"Are you on to the timetable yet?" asked a tall detective in the front row.

"I'll get to that," Kate said. Her voice remained calm.

"What about the survivor?" another officer asked.

Cole was about to intervene when Kate took control of the situation. He felt protective, though he didn't know why. She had demonstrated an adept ability to take care of herself. Maybe that was the problem: she didn't need him one damn bit.

"Save your enthusiasm for the field investigation," she said. "At the end of my presentation, I'll accept questions."

"He had to physically carry the most recent victim to another location to hang her," the same uniform persisted.

"The execution of the crimes gives him added physical strength. Adrenaline is a factor."

Gradually, the rumbling quieted down. That's when Cole heard Grace speaking.

"She possesses a certain instinctive ease. Not surprising. In her position, she's used to dealing with a level of mentality that, despite its vehement defenders in the mental-health professions, is evil."

Cole could never be certain when Grace's statements were intended as compliments. But he quietly agreed that Kate was skilled at this business of crawling inside the heads of serial killers.

"The setup of the most recent crime," Kate was saying, "was that of an organized killer, a cool individual in complete control." She paused. "But something went wrong. His reaction was that of an unorganized offender."

For a moment, Cole pressed the heels of his hands against his eyes, but he continued to listen—intently.

"She's good, this one," Grace whispered.

Cole nodded his agreement. *Damn good.*

"I don't suppose a profession like hers leaves time for many quiet meals?"

"You'll have to ask her, Gracie."

She only lifted a brow, and he smiled.

"You like her," the reporter declared.

Cole pressed his lips together and fixed his gaze on Grace. She had him sweating. That wasn't too hard to do, because these days he was standing too close to the fire.

"You don't have anything to say?" she pressed.

"Nope."

"Guess that explains a couple of things."

Grace was an expert at drawing reactions from people. Though he had trouble accepting it, Cole was no exception.

"Like what?" He was smoldering. "What things?"

Grace slowly looked over at him. "You really want to know?"

"I think I should."

"There's talk that the mayor might turn the investigation over to the AG's office." Grace threw her hands up to pat at the air. "My, my. If the mayor knew I was telling you this, he'd stonewall me."

"Yesterday's news," Cole said, dismissively. He'd called in his favor from the redhead.

"He called me aside for a little chat. Said he and some of the brass are clamping down on the leaks. He asked me to keep him informed about what you're spreading."

"Me?"

He was looking at Kate.

"She's a breed apart," Grace declared, redirecting the conversation, "this one."

"Remember," Kate was saying, "the organized murderer is intelligent. Skilled in his occupation. Likely to think about and plan his crime. Likely to be angry and depressed at the time of the murder. Likely to have a precipitating stress over a variety of things including money, employment, and women. And likely to follow events in the media."

In the filled-to-capacity theater, one of the officers told Kate that she'd just described half of the male work force in San Domingo.

"Exactly," she responded. "Look for the guy next door. Serial killers don't wear identifying badges. But they are often fascinated with law enforcement," she warned, "and in their attempt to become identified with the profession, they pose as law-enforcement officers, holding positions such as security guards or auxiliary police."

"What's the motive?" Grace's voice rang out with a crucial question.

It gave Kate pause.

"Motivation is a difficult factor to determine. It requires dealing with the inner thoughts and behavior of the offender. *How* a crime is committed is much more revealing than *why*," Kate continued. "But there is every indication that his motivation for murder is a complex developmental process based on various needs for dominance. I'd speculate that the killer is murdering for power because of some—" Kate broke off abruptly, circling the air with her hands, in search of the right words "—some self-proclaimed sense of entitlement."

"Do the postmortem hangings indicate a need to punish?" someone from the audience asked.

"Not necessarily," Kate said. "If the offender wanted to punish the victims, there would be antemortem evidence of it." There was silence. "The subsequent hangings still puzzle me."

"A deranged serial killer?" someone else asked.

"It would be fair to say that the two are synonymous."

"How can you be sure strangulation didn't occur first in the victims?" Grace called out.

She was a third of the way down the aisle before Cole could stop her.

"Isn't it extremely easy to confuse postmortem changes due to decomposition? Can't postmortem decomposition obliterate subtle signs of true asphyxiation, making it impossible to prove by postmortem examination that strangulation didn't take place?"

Grace was fishing. Cole knew it. So did Kate. He read as much from the expression on Kate's face. But she was holding her own with the toughest news vulture in the city. Cole could see how good Kate was at her work.

"That's a possibility," Kate answered. "But molting of the victims' blood tells us that they were still alive when shot. As the bodies are hung so soon after the shooting, bruising isn't a determining factor."

"Is the offender trying to shock by hanging the victims?" Grace asked.

"Sadism doesn't appear to motivate our perp," Kate said, but before she could continue, there was an uproar from the audience. "Allow me to finish," she said.

"All right, people," Cole interjected. "Agent Quin said quiet."

Kate studied her notes.

"The fact that he hangs his victims postmortem indicates he's attempting to humiliate them," Kate went on, "displaying a lack of respect. On the other hand, that he tidies up the bodies, much as a caring person would do, contradicts that."

It was just another piece that wasn't fitting with anything else yet. There was another rush of questions.

"Which is it?" someone in the audience asked.

"I think he's demonstrating remorse." She paused. "Quiet... quiet, please." A hush fell. "I'll take one more question."

"Is it true," Grace said, lifting her voice an octave, "that your profile depends on there being interaction between the offender and victim?"

"It's true that interaction usually takes place," Kate conceded, "but there are no absolutes in this business." She then stacked her papers, thanked everyone for coming, and walked off the stage.

Cole gave Kate a thumbs-up. Within minutes he was out in the lobby with Grace, waiting for Kate, straining to look for her.

Despite the task that confronted him in the next few days and weeks, he couldn't help the smile that lifted his heart. Filled with renewed confidence, he knew that he and Kate, together, could find the serial killer.

THERE WERE TWO THINGS Kate didn't want to do at the moment. The first was matching wits with Detective Grasso. The second was figuring out whether Simon LaRoush was skilled in repartee. But she was flanked by both men as she made her way up the aisle toward the lobby.

"It seems to me that you're giving way too much consideration to a psychopath," Simon was saying.

"I thought that was the idea, Prosecutor," Kate replied, trying hard not to take exception, but it seemed as though Simon was going out of his way to knock her off-balance.

"Once you understand what's going on with him," Scoot put in, "tracking him gets easier."

She saw the surprise, the distrust, on Simon's face.

"You're a shrink?" Simon asked her.

"A behavioral-science . . . agent," she told him, rethinking the expert business.

LaRoush seemed beaten down by life, bitter. At best he was pitiable, and Kate was relieved to reach the lobby where she spotted Cole waiting with Grace.

"The Chief tells me you're here to save a handful of human lives," Simon said, speaking with a cigarette clenched between his teeth.

"I'll do all I can to help out," she said.

Smoke curled about his body, hovering, giving the impression that he'd just arrived by way of a magic lamp.

"You're in an interesting mood, Simon," Scoot said.

"This case is not my heart's desire." Simon spoke to Kate, ignoring Scoot entirely. Smoke streamed from the prosecutor's nose.

"But you'll handle it?" Kate asked, realizing Simon was coy, not stupid.

"Here's a guy who enjoys putting offenders behind bars for as long as the law will allow," Scoot bellowed for every ear in the lobby to hear.

Simon's temper was coiled and ready to strike.

"What's the big deal?" he argued. His pasty face split into a frown. "Once they cross the line, they're fair game."

Kate needed to lead a dialogue with Simon LaRoush, but not now.

"Will the two of you excuse me?" she asked politely.

She didn't look back when she walked away.

"Well done, Kate," Grace drawled at her approach, throwing a brief smile in her direction.

"I didn't expect to find you here," Kate said, forcing a calm tone.

"You'll find me where the news is at."

"Glad you could make it," Kate returned, glimpsing Cole.

He was looking directly at her. His eyes held compassion that another time might have dissipated her aggravation. But she wasn't going to make the mistake of trusting him a second time today.

"You just showed me how badly I needed a fed," Cole murmured. "The profile was stunning."

"They usually are," Kate said. "It's always exciting to dissect a madman."

"Did Cole brief you on my media idea?" Grace pressed on. "He assured me I would have your full cooperation. Was he right?"

Kate's control was slipping fast, with anger dangerously close. "That depends," she countered. "Why don't you tell me what this is all about?"

She was beginning to think all reporters were pseudo Columbos. The reporter leveled her turquoise eyes at Kate when Cole's beeper went off. He didn't appear pleased.

"Considering the status of the investigation," Grace said, ignoring the noise, "I'm proposing a plan to spoon-feed select information to the killer, information to lead him to believe that a solution is close at hand—"

Cole's beeper persisted until finally he had to excuse himself. Kate saw a flicker of something in his eyes as he looked at her.

"You might want to rethink the newspaper angle," Kate said to the reporter, feeling tension coil in her neck.

"What for?"

"Sometimes that kind of thing backfires. Sending false signals could interfere with the emotional cool-down phase. His disposition won't differ too much from that of a bear being forced out of hibernation."

"Now, how bad can that be?" Grace asked in a singsong voice, while Kate looked on with irritation. "At least something will be happening in an investigation gone sour."

"You've laid out a blueprint for a time bomb," Kate said. "I tend to get a little edgy about the use of psychological approaches to create or compound stress, rather than relieve it."

"I thought that was your job."

"I'm here doing my job," Kate said. Grace's face distorted into a false look of concern. "A fresh crime scene at Lake Pleasant is icing up by the minute."

A single exaggerated blink from Grace told her she had sounded convincing. Grace nodded knowingly.

"Kate, my dear, much obliged," she said, moving toward the door. She practically ran over Cole. "We'll talk soon."

"Where's she going?" Cole asked.

Kate stuck her tongue in her cheek for a moment. Then she said, "To a fresh crime scene."

Cole froze with his coffee cup halfway to his lips. "A...what?"

Chapter Fourteen

Despite the turmoil in his heart over Kate, Cole still had a madman on the loose in San Domingo. Kate was angry with him. So was the mayor. And Scoot. He had a stalled investigation and a surviving victim barely clinging to life. He was seated behind his desk, turned to face the window. Outside, rush-hour traffic was winding down. He wheeled his chair around, locked his file cabinets, then pushed himself upright.

What would it really be like to share a life with Kate? he wondered, tentatively trying to imagine something he hadn't let himself consider until now. Even if she could reconcile herself to his ambiguous beginnings, to the secrets of his childhood, could he? Wouldn't it be worse to spend his life wondering what could have been?

He'd spent more time in Kate's company during the past two days than he had during the past year and a half. It made him more acutely aware of his desire for her than he thought he could bear, but rather than destroy their rapport with any more antagonism over their respective professions, he would wait until the investigation was resolved.

He was drawn from his self-defeating thoughts by a detective bidding him good-night at his office door.

"Pulling a double, Chief?"

"Just on my way out," Cole said, matching the young man's nod.

His watch read six o'clock. Shift change was past, the offices had emptied, and he was grateful for the privacy. On his way to the parking lot, he nodded at two more passing uniformed officers, then strode through the back door.

Winter continued to strangle the life out of spring, with record low temperatures. In seconds, he was driving down the busy boulevard where he was able to mesh with the rest of the crowded city. He found the anonymity soothing. Nobody to offer condolences. Nobody to question his movements. For the time being, he'd managed to escape the notoriety of being the police chief with a serial killer a jump ahead of him.

Not even the heavy traffic could deter him. His apartment was part of a mini high rise in the overrated San Domingo foothills. He'd depleted his savings account to buy it nearly two years ago. After Kate left, he'd needed a change. He'd wanted no memories, nothing familiar, nothing to remind him of what could have been. "It's not home," Libby had told him. He'd smiled and said that was exactly the point.

To his surprise, he'd gotten comfortable there. He was putting down roots. The potted plant he'd bought for the kitchen windowsill was thriving. A cat named

Chin Chin held down the fort while he was away. On this particular evening, he was especially grateful for the home away from home.

Cole turned off the engine of the Caprice.

"Damn," he murmured, considering the multitude of issues needing to be resolved. He was doing all he could, but the thought brought no comfort.

Moments later he let himself into his apartment. Chin Chin was the doorkeeper, but tonight the gray feline was nowhere to be found. More accustomed to the welcoming committee than he'd realized, he missed the cat's conspicuously absent loyalty tonight. The few things that Cole cared anything about were deserting him en masse.

He jerked off his tie, slipped out of his jacket, then strode into the kitchen. He poured himself a shot of Scotch and downed it. His eyes teared and his throat burned. He choked back a coughing sensation while he waited for the liquor to numb him. He wasn't sure that more alcohol would help, but he took another stiff belt, anyway.

He opened a can of crabmeat for Chin Chin, and was applying a generous dollop of sour cream when he heard someone moving about in the living room. He drew his weapon and pressed it across his breast as though he were going to recite the pledge of allegiance.

"What a worthless fuzzball!" Scoot exclaimed as he rounded the corner and dropped Chin Chin on the countertop.

Cole's heart lurched into his throat for a moment.

"Damn!" he snapped. "You nearly got yourself shot." Cole was too shaken to pay any attention to Chin Chin.

"I hate cats," Scoot griped. "Allergic to them. They belong in a jungle with claws like that. All of them. Cockroaches, too. They refuse to die. Did you know that? Pesticides don't kill them anymore."

"You might have called first."

"I did. You weren't here, so I used the key you gave me for checking on the fuzzball. Remember?" Scoot pointed the shiny object at Cole as if it was a gun.

"I didn't expect you to just show up one day, wearing an apron. You look silly in that thing. And you never told me you hated cats."

Cole laid his snub-nosed .38 on the countertop, then leaned over it himself, forcing down the urge to empty his stomach. At this point, there was not a lot that could shake him up, except that he'd been indulging his nerves for more than a week now and had put away enough antacid tablets to calcify his entire body.

"Thought you might need some company." Scoot paused then, digging in his pocket for his lighter.

"Thought you were going to quit," Cole said, impatience in his tone.

"I did quit smoking—inside. You didn't say nothing about outside." He gripped the lighter while he poured himself a slug of Scotch. "Coming?" his C of D asked, pointing the glass toward the French doors leading to the balcony.

No was not an option, given Scoot's tenacity. But he was equally as loyal, and Cole sometimes thought that's what he liked most about the stubborn detective.

"Go ahead, I'll be there in a minute."

Cole had been trying to make sense of the events of the past few days. He neither wanted nor needed Scoot's good intentions. He choked down his third drink, then went into a coughing fit. His throat burned like fire, and his eyes teared. Damn booze was strong enough to kill a horse. He headed for the patio where he would listen to whatever it was Scoot wanted to say, then send him packing. He appreciated Scoot's concern, but he needed to be alone. His sidekick was invading his private refuge.

"We're having a damn cookout?" Cole blurted when he stepped outside. "You could have asked."

"Like I said, you weren't wearing your pager."

Cole turned his eyes toward the fire on the grill. "Who else did you invite?"

Scoot got out another cigarette and pointed with it. "You ain't going to last long the way you're eating. A pound of protein ought to feed your brain. It'll help you to think."

Cole nodded at Scoot, too drained to feel any way but indifferent. Maybe the detective was right. He couldn't remember his last meal. And he definitely wasn't thinking straight. Besides, Scoot had something on his mind. He was a no-nonsense kind of man who usually said his piece and left.

"Belly up," Scoot said.

Cole did, of course. Besides, the steaks smelled good enough to eat, reminding him that he really was hungry. And Scoot had gone all out to make garlic toast topped with Parmesan cheese, fresh pineapple chunks, and pasta with parsley butter—not a menu Cole would have conjured up, but appetizing nonetheless. He ate. When they'd finished, Scoot reached for another cigarette. He was about to spill what was on his mind.

"I got this theory," he said, pushing away from the table. "See, I think—"

The clanging telephone was music to Cole's ears. He'd been spared. For a moment.

"Cole!" Kate's voice sounded desperate. "Thank God you're home."

"What is it? What's wrong?"

"The victim woke up from her coma tonight."

There was an audible silence.

"Damn." A layer of tension dissolved. A new one was building. He heard background noises, voices and intercoms. He took a long breath. "Where are you?"

"At the hospital."

"Have you talked to her?"

"Not yet. I'm waiting for you."

"I'm on my way."

Cole said goodbye, dropped the receiver back into the cradle with a clatter, and turned around to regard Scoot.

"What the hell was that all about?" his C of D barked.

Cole let the mystery of the moment dangle like bait on a hook.

"What I *ain't* gonna do is play twenty questions with you."

"Try this on for size. Phyllis Coffer woke up tonight." Cole held up a hand. "Don't just stand there with your chin on the floor. Say something." He slapped Scoot on the arm. His chief detective stood a bit straighter as he absorbed the news.

"Son of a bitch—did she talk?" the detective asked. "Tell me. What'd she say?"

"Come on. You can ride over with me to find out."

"No...I've got the brown 'bomb.'"

"Suit yourself." Cole was halfway across the living room. "See you there. The big one's going down."

"IS IT TRUE?" Cole asked, striding down the hospital corridor toward Kate.

She nodded briefly and bit her lower lip. Cole seemed to notice her unusual silence. A small frown creased his brow as he stopped in front of her, so close she could feel his breath.

"We need to talk," she said in a gentle voice.

Inside, she was breaking apart. *The professional at work,* Kate thought, pain squeezing her chest.

She took his hand, urging him into a private lounge a short distance from Phyllis Coffer's room. Whatever his reaction, she thought, she would be there for him, help him work through it, as he had done with her, when she had lost her parents. For the time being, at least, all thoughts of not trusting him flew out the window, along with her sense of self-preservation.

"What's happened?" he queried.

"Phyllis Coffer is awake," she began softly.

There was no easy way to tell him. She looked at him through a blur of tears. Cole's hands framed her face.

"What's wrong?" he murmured, pushing a tear from her cheek with his thumb. "You make it sound like bad news."

Her muscles tensed. Her heart raced. Adrenaline pumped her up for the bleakest moment in her life.

"She identified her assailant...."

"Go on."

Kate knew that what she had to tell him would not give him relief or peace of mind. Tears filled her eyes. There was nothing else to focus on so she got right to the point, choosing her words with painstaking care.

"She swears that the man who shot her—" She broke off, paralyzed with dread. "Phyllis Coffer identified your father—Judge McGuire."

Cole's eyes were riveted on hers, but he didn't hear her words. His arms dropped to his sides, and he took a step backward. His hands coiled into fists. He took another step, then dropped onto a couch. Still he held Kate in his cold scrutiny. Quiet fell between them like a thick fog. Cole wet his lips, then stretched his mouth into a sick smile.

"Kate...what are you saying? You expect me to believe—"

He had backed off just enough for her to realize he was much more man now, than cop.

"Cole, please don't think I wanted the investigation to end this way."

"I can't think—but I know the Judge didn't kill those people. We need to look harder. We'll find something else."

She still held out hope of finding the answering-machine tape, but the possibility that it would resurface and provide evidence to exonerate the Judge, looked bleak, indeed.

"I wish I could tell you something else, but you deserved to hear the truth.... Try to understand."

He sat, paralyzed, for no more than a split second, while reality kicked in. She had just destroyed him.

"Well, I do understand," he snapped, jumping up. "She's mistaken."

Kate felt as if she had a gun to her head. She needed time to think, time to weigh one loss against another.

"I thought it would be over when we discovered the truth," she said, her voice unsteady. "I thought I could finish my profile and just wash my hands of it. But it never ends. It just gets uglier and uglier."

"Who knows about this?"

"The two of us—"

"And Phyllis Coffer."

The hurt on his face broke her heart.

"I'm so sorry," she whispered.

He leaned his head against hers and closed his eyes, struggling to keep his volatile emotions from getting out of hand. She widened her eyes to keep from breaking into tears. This couldn't be happening.

"This is crazy," Cole muttered. "There has to be some logical explanation. The Judge tried her case—

why wouldn't he be the last face she remembers? Vindictive behavior isn't uncommon."

There were two solid leads to fall back on—matching the bullets to Judge McGuire's revolver, and typing his blood to the sample taken from the victim's clothing. Judge McGuire's revolver was missing and presumed stolen. The realization hit Kate with the force of a sledgehammer.

"Cole, don't do this to yourself," she consoled, aware that this wasn't the time to mention damning evidence.

"That's it? No discussion? Nothing?"

"We have to proceed just as we would with any other case."

"The Judge hasn't killed anybody," he refuted, each word uttered with great clarity.

"He'll face a jury—" Kate said softly.

"He didn't do it," Cole repeated. "You've got it all wrong. You'll find something else."

"I'm doing everything I can to get to the truth."

"You aren't looking hard enough!"

Rare tears glistened in Cole's eyes. He tried to swallow his emotion. For a moment, he just stood, looking down. Slowly, he turned to leave.

"Where are you going?" Kate followed him to the door. "I'm going with you."

"No," he said, his tone as dead as the look in his eyes. "Leave me—I want to be alone."

She stood at the door, looking out toward the parking lot while her life was falling apart. She would stand here a moment longer, she told herself, until her strength returned. Until she could figure out what to do next. She sagged against the doorframe. She had all the time in the world.... Don't let him do this again....

"Cole!"

She raced out the door and caught up with him, but emotion caused her body to tremble, and she needed time before she could speak.

"Let's go someplace and talk," she said, wiping a tear from her face and turning away for another moment. She felt her lungs constricting again, but her instincts told her to be totally frank. "Please. We've got to talk this out. I love him, too. There's nothing I've learned tonight that can't wait until tomorrow. Coffer is heavily sedated and under guard."

He sighed deeply and turned to face her, his eyes dark and brooding. She looked down at the white knuckles of his shaking fists.

"I've got to get out of here," he said with a groan.

The sweet ache of relief stole over her as she saw the reluctant acceptance, the tentative opening of the door he'd just slammed in her face.

"Where would you like to go?" she asked, her voice barely a whisper. "Your office? A restaurant? Where?" She was trying to keep her suggestions neutral.

He thought for a moment, then looked down at her, a spark of frantic longing in his eyes. "My apartment," he said in a husky voice.

There was no hesitation on Kate's part. "I'll follow you."

Cole nodded and got into his Caprice. Kate looked at the sky, breathed a great, deep sigh, then headed for her own car.

INSIDE HIS APARTMENT, Cole glanced over at Kate, leaning against the front door, and noticed that her cheeks were pink from the sun. They stared at each other in a moment of truce. A heartrending look of sadness stole across her face. Her eyes misted. Neither had uttered a word. It seemed that she was waiting, compassionately biding her time until he gave her the go-ahead.

"Kate... you're the only one..."

He wondered at the twist in his chest at the simple utterance of her name. The rest wouldn't come. But if he couldn't tell her that only her love for him could block out the pain, he could show her. For the first time in eighteen months, Cole silently admitted to the extent of his love for Kate. He was overwhelmed by the unrelenting urge to hold her in his arms and crush her against him until their emotions changed from pain to passion. His heart beat with the force of a jackhammer.

Cole's long strides closed the distance separating them. He lifted her to carry her to the bedroom, then gently placed her on the bed. He slipped her sweater over her head, then he pulled off her jeans, leaving her lacy underwear for later. In seconds he was naked and sliding into her waiting arms. Now, he covered the distance of eighteen months simply by reaching across the bed for her.

"Cole," she began, locking her legs around him, "I want—"

"Shh," he cut in. "I know what you want...."

He wanted it, too, the soul-deep intimacy that occurred only when two people were deeply in love. No inhibitions, no repressions. Moments later, they were joined. Twice, before she fell asleep, he poured himself—his nonverbal emotions—into her.

With Kate close by, sleeping soundly, he lay on his bed, staring at the ceiling. Though she was inches away, he felt more alone than he had in years. The feeling was so similar to the one he'd experienced during his childhood, when he was in the foster-care agency, without a family. The loneliness had been suffocating.

The bedside phone rang, startling them both. It was Scoot babbling on the other end of the line, something about an officer down.

Kate sat up as Cole hurried to his closet, yanked a shirt off a hanger, and started to dress.

"What happened?" she asked him.

"Scoot is sitting on a nasty one. Wants me to have a look."

Cole shrugged into his leather jacket, then hurried around the end of the bed to kiss Kate quickly before starting away. He had reached the bedroom door before she spoke.

"We have to talk." Her voice was gentle but unyielding. "Let me tell the Judge."

"No, I can't do that." He stood with his hand on the door, facing away.

"It's better that way," she argued. "He'll need you later. Libby will need you."

After a silence, Cole straightened decisively. He still could not look at her. "I need some time to think this through—before you move on it."

"All right. Just don't take too long."

THE MAYOR HAD BEEN right. The case was filled with conflicts of interest, including hers. And Kate knew her conflict was larger than her heart could contain. She loved the McGuires—*all* the McGuires. But she also had a job to do. She hadn't heard from Cole since last night.

For the rest of her life, she would have to live with her decision to proceed with the arrest. She could only hope that, in Cole's despair, he secretly wanted her to relieve him of this burden. Kate prayed that in some small way, even while executing her duty, she might alleviate some of their pain.

But as she eased her car down the driveway to Judge McGuire's home, the unfolding revelation forced her to reexamine her ambitions and desires. She was going to do her job, and because of that, lives were about to change forever.

The blinds were drawn inside the dimly lit Arizona room. Judge McGuire sat alone, staring, his iron gray hair in disarray. His face appeared deeply lined, his melancholy features those of a man who had hoped for the best but received the worst.

"Hello, Your Honor," Kate said gently.

He fixed his eyes on her, but said nothing.

"Where's Libby?" she asked.

"Dressing."

Something in his tone alerted her. For a moment he was silent. Defeated. Kate had never felt such despair in her life.

"Sit down," he said faintly.

There was no hurry now. Whatever his reasons, he was sick, she understood that.

"I have bad news."

"I see."

"Do you want to talk?" she asked.

"I've been told I'm a very good listener."

"Phyllis Coffer woke up tonight."

"I see."

"She identified you as her assailant."

He nodded.

"Why did you send the notes?"

"Notes?"

"The warning notes... Why did you send them?"

"You haven't asked me if I committed those heinous crimes."

"You've been accused.... That's what we need to address."

"You would have made a good criminal-defense attorney, my dear. The successful formula for every criminal lawyer is to never ask your client if he did it."

He looked out the window, as though distracted by the brightness of the day. Kate realized this might be her only chance at achieving answers. The more time that passed, the less chance there was that he would talk.

"Want to talk about this?"

"I admire you, Kate . . . but we're on different sides now. I haven't been advised of my rights yet, and there's no lawyer-client privilege here."

His words, the manner in which he spoke them, with tears in his eyes, sorrowfully, penetrated her heart. Only then did she understand that the truth might never reveal itself.

"Are you ready?" Kate asked with the gentleness she would extend to a child.

"First someone must see to Libby. I don't believe I'm up to it."

"Of course," Kate agreed.

She stood and walked down the hall to a closed door. Opening it, she spoke gently. "Libby?"

Kate found her lying on top of the bedcovers, her eyes searching the ceiling above. Gleaming tracks of tears ran back into her cropped hair. She made no move as Kate entered and crossed to stand by the edge of the bed.

"I realize this is traumatic for you. I want to help if I can."

Libby remained in her same distracted attitude, her gaze still fixed on the ceiling when she spoke. "There's nothing more you can do."

Kate took a seat on a chair opposite the bed, leaned forward, and planted her elbows on her knees. "Maybe there is. The Judge is going to need an attorney."

Libby sat upright as if she'd been jerked. "You'd do that?"

Kate nodded. "Why wouldn't I want to help?"

Libby drained her glass of vodka while shaking off the question. "I'm going downtown with him."

She wobbled her way over to her walk-in closet. Kate followed her. The meticulously organized contents of the wardrobe room ran the length of one entire wall. Inside, there stretched an expanse of neatly pressed pants organized by color, stiff white shirts, and Libby's dresses.

"You've been a loyal friend, Kate," Libby said, slurring her words.

"You don't have to do this." Kate felt her lips trembling. "The Judge would feel better about it if you remained here—to avoid the press."

The sound that erupted so suddenly from Libby's throat sounded like something from a wild animal. Then there was silence. Only from her jerking body could Kate determine that she was sobbing. Gently, she steered her back to the bed.

"Cole's on his way. I called and left a message for him to drive up here. Will you be all right?"

Of course not. None of them were all right. And things would never be the same again.

Chapter Fifteen

The vultures descended as soon as Kate and the Judge exited her car. Halogen lights glared brightly above the television cameras. Heads down, they hurried through the rear door of the police station. With flashbulbs popping and microphones in position, reporters were waiting eagerly for their victim, scavengers descending to draw an admission of guilt from the Judge. As though it were a malignant tumor.

"Keep your head down," Kate said to the Judge. She spoke rapidly, confidently. "It won't be easy, but we'll get through this."

She wasn't so sure about that. She couldn't shake the intuition that something wasn't right about the Judge's behavior. He had simply checked out. As if he was playing the role of a prisoner with a noose around his neck.

"I'll be fine," the Judge said calmly without meeting her eyes.

She'd known the family for a long time, had seen Cole's father under stress before, but today there was something in his demeanor that she couldn't put her finger on.

"Let's go, then," she told him.

Simon LaRoush met them in the hallway.

"I'm going to put him away for life," Simon said, shattering Kate's facade of control.

"Keep going," she urged the Judge.

The possibility that Simon could very well do just that constricted Kate's heart. Her pulse raced. "Not without a confession," she reminded Simon. "He'll be exonerated when the matter reaches the preliminary hearing." Kate shook her head and regarded the prosecutor. "Now get out of our way."

She was thinking clearly again. She and the Judge moved forward, Simon trailing behind them.

"Whose side are you on, Agent Quin? Or has your relationship with Chief McGuire clouded your judgment?"

Simon's words pelted her like stones. She could feel her cheeks blazing. "You bastard," she whispered. "My relationship with Chief McGuire is none of your business."

"It became my business when you brought his father in for murder."

"Let's get something straight," Kate retorted without missing a step. "The jury will make that decision—whether you like it or not." She drove him down a notch with the intensity of her gaze alone. "Now get lost, Simon, unless you've got an arrest warrant. Come on," she said to the Judge.

"Make him comfortable," Simon said, waving the appropriate warrant under her nose. "He's going to be here for some time."

"Don't plan on lubricating your career with this case," Kate warned, "because you've got a conflict of interest the size of Florida."

"Speaking of conflicts," Simon said, "better have your chief of police examine his own." A surge of panic shot through Kate. "I hate to be the one to bust up a cozy arrangement, but the AG has a problem with the chief of police investigating his own father on murder charges."

"This is ridiculous," she said, all innocence. "You're making a mistake, but I figure you're smart enough to see it for yourself."

Simon's was a disgusting smile. His teeth looked like old piano keys, once ivory, but now variegated with shades of brown and yellow.

"I'm sorry you feel that way, Kate."

Kate picked up the pace. So did Simon.

"There's an interesting rumor being bandied about—one that has you extending confidentiality through the lawyer-client privilege cloak to Judge McGuire."

Kate halted abruptly. The sickening smile was still on his face.

"You understand what I'm saying?"

"I've been reading law books since I was three years old," she said with deadly calm. "And understanding them."

Kate gently squeezed the Judge's hand just before she handed him over to the booking sergeant who led him away.

"I'll see you and your friends in court," Simon said with a tone that belied his rage. "The charge is *murder in the first degree.*"

"Oh, God," Kate mumbled.

That only meant one thing. Phyllis Coffer had died.

"Kate?"

Cole's voice was almost unrecognizable. His eyes bore the frightened look of a wild, cornered animal.

"How could you?" he whispered. "I trusted you."

His eyes turned cold now, like ice.

"I did what I had to do," Kate said, but the declaration brought no comfort.

"Gotta watch out for these feds, Chief," Simon interjected. "They can't be trusted. All of 'em, operating on ego."

Simon left them alone then, Cole gaping at Kate, Kate looking regretfully at him.

"There wasn't a choice.... If there had been, I would have gladly welcomed another way out of this. I did what I had to do."

"Brilliant work, Agent Quin," Cole said. "You came out on top—head of the class."

He had every right. Wasn't that what she had wanted? Wasn't that her secret weapon?

Cole turned away from her and walked toward the door.

"Don't do this," Kate whispered.

"*Me?* Consider the score even. Now go and find somebody else's life to ruin!"

THE PATIO LOOKED eerily deserted when Kate slipped into the pool. Time stood on the plus side of eleven o'clock. With a heavy heart, she began a series of unforgiving laps. Harder and harder she pushed herself. Until she felt burning pain. Until her lungs felt as if they might explode.

Find somebody else's life to ruin!

Was that what she was doing? she asked herself. Was she ruining the McGuire family? She swam frantically back and forth, back and forth.

It had been impossible for Kate to manage the conflict of her feelings for Cole and her duty to arrest the Judge. Cole had trusted her—she had betrayed that trust. Cole hated her now, and she couldn't blame him. She'd been so damned filled with that sense of responsibility, that she'd chosen to ignore instinct. *Stop it!* Kate berated herself. The investigation was all that mattered. *Forget Cole McGuire,* she told herself. *You've got a job to do, even if he can't see that.*

Brilliant work, Cole had snapped. *You came out on top—head of the class.*

Kate's life had become a lesson in extremes. The stress from the proceedings had left her feeling lame. She'd racked her brain trying to dig to the truth. The pain of unshed tears formed a lump in her throat. The fury in her strokes eased until, reaching the end of the pool, she barely had the strength to pull herself out of the water.

Tears spilled over her bottom lashes. She pressed her lips together, but the lump in her throat expanded. Collapsed on the deck, she buried her face in her arms and gave in to the torrent of emotion that had been building for days. The violent sobbing eventually spent itself. She sat up and hugged her knees. *Can it just end like this?* she wondered bleakly.

A hastily convened grand jury had indicted the Judge. His "not guilty" plea had the state scrambling to put together an efficient trial. He was absolutely without fear. Except to relate to Kate that nothing could save him, he wasn't talking. No one was talking. Libby was incapacitated by her depression. Kate had never doubted Libby's devotion to the Judge and her family, but seeing Cole's mother in this fragile, broken condition cut to the bone. Cole had distanced himself without another word.

She had taken his father into custody after he had asked her not to. He had trusted her not to. She'd violated his trust. But compromising her integrity posed a worse threat to Kate.

No, she thought miserably. *It can't be over. Not like this.* Somewhere there had to be concrete answers—about the Judge, about the case.

There were many pieces still missing. The prosecution had no weapon. The Judge had reported the .38 stolen after the break-in. The Judge's blood type didn't match with the sample found on the victim's clothing. Nor had the lab been able to match his prints to any in the case files. Not even the voice tape was a clear match.

All they had was Phyllis Coffer's identification of Judge McGuire. Based on that, he would certainly be convicted of capital murder. She could move heaven and earth, and nothing would change that miserable fact.

Kate couldn't shake an inexplicable feeling that the pieces they *did* have were all part of the same puzzle. Not that she could put her finger on any one thing. But if she could have, she realized it would have been the Judge's behavior. The alleged charges were affecting him in a way she did not understand. He had isolated himself mentally, inflicting the cruelest of all punishments on himself, as though treating his ordeal like martyrdom. That kind of behavior was out of character for the Judge.

Desperately Kate embraced the possibility that Cole was right about his father's innocence. She was going for broke. She refused to give up another McGuire.

COLE GLANCED AT KATE inside the courtroom, then quickly, deliberately, looked away. His anger had reached a fever pitch before it had settled into this dull ache inside his heart. Anger for what Kate had done to him, and for what she was doing to his father and his mother. She had betrayed him—and that hurt more than anything else.

If it wasn't for Kate, his mother wouldn't be on the verge of a breakdown, his father wouldn't be standing in this courtroom today.

He looked over at his father, standing rigidly beside Kate. A sudden thought stopped him cold. Had

Kate saved them all the inevitable pain of arrest? Had she kept him from carrying out that unthinkable deed on his own father?

But what did that matter? She'd had no right. No right at all. Whatever they had shared was over, just not meant to be, Cole thought, turning his attention to the jury foreman.

Voir dire had been accomplished in just over two weeks. Jury selection had probably set a record, Cole thought, all because presiding Judge Graham had put the defense attorney on notice at the request of Prosecutor Simon LaRoush. San Domingo remained in an uproar over the Judge's sensitive position, and the speed at which things were handled was whirlwind. The trial was in session for a mere five days when closing arguments were presented and the case went for deliberation to the jury.

And now, the verdict was in. The jury had been out a mere six and a half hours.

"All rise!" the bailiff called out, announcing the grand entrance of presiding Judge Graham.

The robed jurist swept into the courtroom to take his seat behind the bench to receive the verdict in the capital murder of Phyllis Coffer.

Cole looked briefly at his father, deliberately ignoring any eye contact with Kate. She was standing by the Judge, who stood slightly hunched, hands folded in front of him, next to his court-appointed attorney. Cole watched Kate quickly squeeze Judge McGuire's arm.

He had yet to come to terms with his hurt and anger over Kate's actions. But in spite of his defiance, not much else seemed to matter when she was fading from his life. But he wouldn't think about Kate now. Not when the same system his father had believed in was about to turn on him and devour him.

And not when Libby was about to snap. At home she was demonstrating all the signs of a breakdown. Cole was doing his best to comfort her, but she was growing increasingly distant. His mother had always been a strong woman, quick to shun pity, or pats on the back. This entire affair had overwhelmed her. She refused to face the situation. He understood that. He wanted to run from it, too.

The jurors, as they took their seats, looked across at his father, whose head had remained bowed throughout the entire proceedings.

"Has the jury reached a verdict?" The judge's deep voice bounced off the walls inside the courtroom.

"We have, Your Honor," the jury foreman replied.

The deputy clerk accepted the slip of paper from the foreman and delivered it to the judge who silently read it. Cole tried to read his expression, but couldn't. The judge returned the piece of paper to his clerk who strode across the room toward the jury foreman.

"Read the verdict," the judge ordered.

Cole wanted to think of other things. Anything. Kate's eyes were boring holes through him. He felt them on him as surely as if she were stabbing him in the back. And she had, as far as he was concerned.

"In the matter of the State versus David O. McGuire, we, the jury, find the defendant *guilty* of murder in the first degree."

Guiltyguiltyguilty...

Cole watched his father standing immobile, without emotion, as though without comprehension. And when the Judge turned toward him, his expression was so stiff and stoic, Cole thought he looked dead. Capital punishment... Dead... *Dead dead dead*...

This can't be happening. Got to get out...

Wanting to run, Cole strode out of the courtroom. Head held high, shoulders very straight, he maneuvered his way through the crowded lobby. Reporters swarmed after him, tugging at his sleeve, bursting with questions. For a moment he was trapped, could not evade them without shoving them aside. They poked microphones at his mouth until anger galvanized him. The atmosphere turned combative.

"Do you think Judge McGuire is guilty, Chief?" shouted a media figure he couldn't see, but whose voice he recognized. The voices, the questions, the idle buzzing, all of it meshed into a loud, blaring noise from which Cole could no longer decipher anything specific. It occurred to him, as he worked his way through the throng of reporters, that his father was the first condemned man he'd ever seen in person. He didn't look like a killer....

Chapter Sixteen

"Kate?"

"It's two o'clock in the morning," Kate said into the telephone receiver. "Who is this?"

"Grace Van Buren," the voice went on. "Have you heard?"

"Heard what?"

"Judge Graham's court stenographer died—heart attack. Along with his body, authorities found ten cats in the house—and *reams* of his court steno tablets."

Kate woke slowly. Once her eyes were open, she snapped on the bedside lamp. Ten days ago, a jury had rendered a "guilty" verdict in Judge McGuire's case. She'd been unhappy with their decision, but she'd accepted it because capital cases were automatically appealed in the state of Arizona. The judge's case was no exception.

"Those cats were all he left behind—them and his yet-to-be-transcribed trial records."

Kate shook her head. "You're not making any sense."

"The appeal has been held up while the stenographer transcribed his notes." Grace spoke rapidly. "Those notes are the only official court records of Judge McGuire's trial."

"So? Someone else transcribes them now," Kate said with a note of disgust in her voice.

"Wrong," Grace retorted with inappropriate glee. "He was a bit of an eccentric, Kate. He didn't use a stenotype machine. He had his own special shorthand. Don't you see?"

"Go on." Kate propped herself up with pillows, wide-awake now.

"*No one* has been able to decipher his notes."

Those were among the most profound words Kate had ever heard. She kept running a hand through her unruly hair. She was almost as nervous as Grace. At any moment, she expected impulse to take over. She had to remind herself that Grace Van Buren was a reporter, and this was a story for her to pursue.

"Kate? Are you there?"

Think.

"Yes, I'm here. But if you don't get to the point, I won't be for long."

"Without the transcription of the trial proceedings," Grace began, "there is no official record of the trial." She was sucking air in gulps. "The star witness is dead."

And there was no weapon or ammunition with which to match the bullet extracted from the victim's head.

"There's speculation Judge Graham will be forced to set the judgment aside without prejudice and ask the prosecutor to refile the charges." There was a dramatic pause. "Think he'll cut the defendant loose?"

"The Judge hasn't been exonerated." The muscles tensed in the back of her neck.

"Well, Kate, what do you say?"

Kate had to force a pragmatic calm into her voice as she replied. "I say we wait."

"I've got no travel plans."

Kate replaced the receiver in its cradle and decided not to fool with the notion of going back to sleep. Defeat seeped through her as she extracted herself from the bed. She knew exactly why Grace demanded a statement from her at this ungodly hour. Kate had listened to her share of boring professors conducting boring law classes. But this was pure, unadulterated high drama. Just what Grace needed to jump-start her career.

Kate was padding into the bathroom to shower when it occurred to her that Cole had to be told. Should she call now—or wait until morning? A hot shower would clear her head. She opened the mirrored linen closet and reached for a clean bath towel. Her hand felt something else. She pulled the object out for inspection.

The tape. From Phyllis Coffer's answering machine—exactly where she had left it. Then fresh towels had been piled on top of it. Her interest piqued, she raced to retrieve Scoot's recorder from the nightstand drawer. Maybe someone else had been after Phyllis

Coffer. Maybe there was something on the tape to exonerate the Judge. Maybe—

There was only one way to get an answer. She waited until the thundering in her chest subsided and her hand steadied. Then she inserted the tape, depressed the Play button. Strange voices filled the silence in her bedroom, saying nothing to seize her attention. Nothing at all. Misery twisted Kate's heart as she admitted the tape offered no new hope for the Judge's case. Tears moistened her cheeks before she realized she was crying.

"It's useless," she whispered, swiping at the teardrops. "Useless..."

COLE WANTED TO TIME travel, but when the elevator lurched to a halt, he had traveled only two floors up. He exited the worthless time machine, his legs feeling like dangling concrete pillars as he forced them to carry him down the hallway, past the secretary's vacant desk and toward the mayor's open office door.

As he neared, the sound of voices floating out into the corridor sprang up like a brick wall. Not just any voices—the mayor's and Kate's. They stopped him cold.

"Everything is at stake," the mayor was saying.

Not an ounce of friendliness lurked under the mayor's facade of authority today, and Cole knew what was about to come.

"All he needs is time," Kate urged. "He'll come around."

"Then you agree that putting him on administrative leave is necessary? He must get his personal life in order."

Kate's momentary silence screamed into Cole's ears. "Is this why you summoned me?" She began in a whisper, but her voice rose steadily. "I've been here for the better part of an hour. Why didn't you tell me this up front?"

"Call it gut instinct," the mayor pressed on, "but I haven't been satisfied with the progress of this investigation from the beginning." He paused, and Cole heard the movements as the mayor flicked a cigarette lighter to flame. "Precisely why I brought you on board, Quin. I could have assigned the investigation to the AG's office, but that could have turned nasty." A pause. "Your job here is finished."

Cole couldn't believe what he was hearing. Kate was selling him out. His heart felt as if it had been torn to pieces.

"Power makes men so predictable," the mayor said coldly.

"Not all of them," Cole said.

The sound of his voice caught Kate's attention, and she snapped her head up. Her eyes widened as she saw him walk into the room. Her mouth tightened into a grim line.

"We weren't expecting you, Chief," the mayor said, inappropriately cheery.

"No...I suppose you weren't," Cole murmured, his gaze sweeping over Kate to include her as a recipient of his reply.

"Cole, what are you doing here?"

"It's best that the chief is here," the mayor broke in. He turned to Cole. "We've got something to tell you."

We? The misery in his heart forced him to manufacture conclusions.

"I've got something to tell you, too," he returned with deadly calm.

DEEP LINES OF FATIGUE etched themselves in the hard planes of Cole's face. Shadows obscured the laugh lines under his bleak eyes. Kate wanted to talk to him, wanted to make him realize that she wasn't cooperating with this lynchman who wanted to place the chief on administrative leave.

"Cole, I want you to understand my position," she said quickly, before he assumed the wrong impression.

Emotion clogged her throat when she met his gaze and saw only pain and grief.

"I thought you were different," he said.

He laughed mirthlessly and went to the mayor's desk to toss down an envelope.

"Give me a chance to explain," she pleaded. There was no time now for anything but honesty.

"I don't need you to connect the dots for me, Kate."

"Please understand," she tried again, feeling the wrenching of emotion in her heart. "I'm just doing my job the best way I know how."

"Duty above all else?"

She felt tears springing to her eyes, and turned away. She swept her hand through her hair.

"I'm sorry, Cole," she murmured.

"For what?" he asked. "For setting me up?"

Shaking his head, he moved to the doorway, leaning against the frame.

"My resignation's in that envelope," he said to neither one of them in particular. "Sometime during the night—"

He broke off abruptly, pressing his lips together, choking back emotion. "The Judge hanged himself."

A moment of startled silence suspended them. The mayor flopped into his desk chair, his protruding eyes bulging like those of an exotic fish. His mouth twitched slightly as he looked at Cole.

"God, no," Kate whispered.

She started to go toward him, but suddenly he ground his teeth and slammed his fist into the doorframe, sending a loud thud echoing throughout the room. Kate jumped.

"You broke him, Kate." He stepped toward her, biting out each word. "Wasn't that the point? Get inside his head and dissect him?"

Kate placed one hand on her stomach and covered her mouth with the other, muffling her sobs. A tear rolled down her cheek. She quickly wiped it away.

"Cole, I'm sorry, so sorry. Maybe my approach was wrong, but—"

"*Wrong?*" he interrupted. "Head of the class *again,* Agent Quin."

Her secret weapon had just blown up in her face.

Briefly, Cole's eyes gravitated back to Kate, his haunted gaze meeting hers as if for the last time. Then he turned his back to her and walked out. He'd slipped through her fingers once and for all.

"No," she cried out, running out the door and into the hallway after him. "I won't let you do this again." She caught his arm, stopping him, and stood before him to look into his eyes. "This isn't about me. It's yourself you don't trust. Stop looking for excuses to blame your fears on everyone else."

"This isn't about fear."

"What, then?" she pleaded. "Talk to me, Cole."

He silenced her with a wave of his hand. "Go away."

"Are you sending me away again?"

"No guilt trips, Kate."

"Then don't toy with me. It's time you figured out what it is you want from me." He remained silent. Kate squeezed her eyes shut. "What *do* you want?"

"I want you to go away—get out of my life—leave me alone."

She did.

WHEN THE ELEVATOR DOORS slid shut, Cole felt as though his fate had been sealed. His world would never be the same again without his parents—without Kate. His heart had been smashed, dissected, much the same way his life had been disassembled.

He had always thought his job made a difference. Police work was all he knew. It was all he'd ever wanted to do. It had been his anchor, the one constant he could depend on—his consolation prize for his lack of family roots. And it had all seemed so simple—enforcing right and wrong—until the bottom had fallen out of his world. Déjà vu. The loneliness was back. He was a nine-year-old boy again. Alone. Without anyone. Helpless to change the shape of his world. Yet his need for love was greater than ever.

DURING THE TWO WEEKS that followed Judge McGuire's funeral, Kate slept more and rested less. The room she'd taken in town was small, cramped. She was as tired as she had ever been. Something about the dream had woken her this time—the dream she'd been having since Cole's father's death. The dream was always about the same sad, neon eyes. No face. No body. Just neon eyes.

For a moment she didn't stir, except to turn her eyes toward the clock on the nightstand. Three o'clock. She had the sense of her ordered life whirling apart. Just getting up in the mornings was an effort.

What can I do? she had asked Cole, feeling desperately helpless at the funeral.

Your job was the Hangman. You did it.

Kate had turned to Libby, seeking and offering comfort, but Libby had stared at her blankly.

She had to pull herself together, Kate had thought, diving back into her work with the vigor of a desperate woman. There were reports to wrap up. She had laid it all on the line, all of it, and lost. There were no winners. Everyone was suffering the emptiness, the loneliness, the uncertainty.

She threw back the covers and swung her legs over the side of the bed. By moonlight she stood, walked over to the dinette table she had been using for a desk, and switched on the overhead lights. A stack of files lay there along with pencils, pens, notepaper. Tidy. Everything in its place. Kate carried the files with her to a comfortable chair where she began scanning the information in them again. The nagging uncertainty of the Judge's guilt or innocence gnawed at her conscience.

She spent the day reviewing the multitude of notes, transcripts and official reports, stopping only once for a quick lunch.

This time, she was looking for answers to several specific questions in the reams of documents. Lab work had determined that only Phyllis Coffer's prints were on the two glasses Kate had confiscated from the victim's bathroom. Another dead end.

There had been two phone calls to 911—minutes apart. The guard had used the lobby phone to make one call. The Judge had allegedly used a public telephone booth just blocks from the courthouse, to make the other call. Kate had listened repeatedly to the recorded calls. They offered nothing beyond the fact that the Judge had disguised his voice to prevent identification. But the blood remained the most puzzling aspect to emerge from the case.

What happened to "beyond a reasonable doubt"? For Kate, reasonable doubt hung in the air like a bad odor.

She'd read the victim's signed statement again and again, but she wanted to see it once more. Maybe the victim had lied... maybe she'd been seeking revenge against Judge McGuire. Maybe she had spoken his name simply because he was the last important person to speak to her preceding the attack.

The weapon was still missing. The bullet had been recovered and matched to those slugs removed from the three previous victims. So why was she wasting her time poring over these files? What was the fly in the ointment? What was the obstruction that had kept her from accepting everything and simply moving on to the final report?

They leave something and they take something with them. Kate caught her lip between her teeth. What remained unexplained was the second blood type found on the victim. A blood sample from the Judge failed to match it. Kate felt overwhelmed by a sudden thought, a thought that brought her thinking to a complete halt.

Three people had been in or around Judge McGuire's office within minutes of the attempted murder. Nan Dupree, Simon LaRoush, and Grace Van Buren. No one had cross-checked their blood with the sample found on the victim's clothing. This was simply a process of elimination, but she knew she wouldn't rest until it had been done. She should hurry. It was nearly five o'clock.

Within minutes, Kate had spoken to the pathologist and arranged for blood samples to be taken from

Simon LaRoush and Grace Van Buren. Nan Dupree wasn't answering her telephone. Kate decided it was time to track her down.

Kate tilted her head back and squeezed her eyes shut for a moment. If she was wrong, the investigation really *would* be over. If she was right, there would still be a high price to pay.

Chapter Seventeen

The house stood in total darkness when Kate arrived. Thunder rumbled from so close above her, she thought she could reach up and touch the night sky. Occasional lightning speared the ground, illuminating what appeared to be grotesque shapes and figures.

Odd, Kate thought, that the house was so dark. Unusual, too, to find the door ajar. Fear sprang up inside her, heightening her senses, slamming her heart against her ribs. She drew her weapon, unsure what to expect, and plunged into the dark interior.

The air was stale and as still as death. She blinked her eyes, attempting to adjust to the pitch black, and tried not to breathe.

With her left arm extended to guide her, and her right hand clutching her gun, she moved across the kitchen in tiny, shuffling steps. *Where?* she wondered.

"I've been waiting for you," came a vaguely familiar voice, the same voice recorded on the 911 call-in tapes.

The sound of a revolver being cocked slammed into Kate's ears like a thunderclap. *From the living room? Wait.* Her eyes were adjusting slowly to the darkness.

"I thought... we could talk," she murmured.

"Yes," the voice said. "I'd like that, but first put your gun away."

Kate still held the weapon, but her hands shook so violently, she wasn't certain she could use it. No. She couldn't do that. *Talk. Find out the truth.*

Feeling her way along, Kate bumped the side of her face on the refrigerator. Her left eye stung. Her heart hammered at her chest until she thought it would split wide open. Lightning struck, and she flinched at the unexpected flash of brightness.

Move! Don't be a stationary target!

"I can't put my gun down." Kate finished speaking, then moved noiselessly aside, realizing the irony even as she did so—if her stalker's eyes had adjusted well enough in the dark to spot Kate's gun, then she was *already* a target.

A loud metallic noise reverberated through the house. At first, Kate was startled. Then she realized it was the sound of the automatic sun shields, sealing off the windows and doors and turning the house into a tomb. Kate's breath caught, and she was shaking so, she doubted she would have the strength to pull the trigger. She sucked in air to help her regain control.

"What does it feel like, Kate?"

"What does *what* feel like?"

"Being dead wrong."

Stall. "I know about the Judge."

"I expect you do."

"I tracked down Nan Dupree earlier this evening."

"There was never an affair."

"You knew?" Kate asked.

"The Judge discussed everything with me."

"Want to talk about it?"

"Nan had been drinking heavily on that final day of Phyllis Coffer's trial. The Judge took her into chambers and threatened to have her disbarred over it."

Kate bit her lip for courage. It drew blood.

"Nan became hysterical. He sent her to the ladies' room. And forgot about her."

Kate could feel the trickle of blood on her chin, but she feared moving her hand to wipe it.

"When Nan returned," Kate began, picking up the story, "she got as far as the anteroom where she overheard the two of you—entrenched in a heated discussion."

"You're a clever girl, Kate, but Nan couldn't have told you anything about Phyllis Coffer, because she was gone by then."

"That's true, but Nan overheard you telling the Judge that you wouldn't protect him any longer. At the time, what you said meant nothing to her. But later, after the news broke about the attempt on Phyllis Coffer's life, she thought the Judge was guilty. She went into hiding, unable to cope in her deteriorating physical condition...."

Kate paused and drew in a trembling breath. "We talked tonight and she gave me enough to work with. I was ready to type my report. Then I realized how I could corroborate her story. I pulled the ribbon cartridge from the typewriter you loaned me. I transcribed the carbon tape, Libby. Your messages were there."

"Anybody could have used that typewriter."

"True enough, but I matched the blood on Phyllis Coffer to your donations at the blood bank."

Let it be over, Kate prayed silently. *Let it be over.* "You're tired, Libby.... Put the gun down. Let me help you."

"I can't. I mustn't leave you here to tell Cole. He's suffered too much. Poor little boy... All he wanted was a family...."

"Put the gun down, Libby, and talk to me," Kate pleaded in a whisper.

"He was nine years old, but he looked six when we saw him for the first time...."

Shaken, Kate considered what Libby had just said. "He never told me."

"I didn't want to hurt either of you. But you wouldn't listen. Why did you persist? I tried to warn you. You don't know what it's like to lose your husband. Every time he set one of them free...he withered a little more. I had to do something. I was losing the person I loved the most—I had to punish those people."

Kate had been tensed for so long now that every muscle in her body burned. She jumped at the sound of a tremendous clap of thunder, then at the noise of the sun shields moving in their tracks. The light that broke through the kitchen window was dim, but the subsequent flash of lightning was enough for Kate to see Libby, arms extended, aiming a revolver at her.

"You do understand, don't you, Kate? Don't you?"

Shoot. Or you'll die. Can't. Kate's right arm snapped up; her fingers closed around the gun. Tears filled her eyes. Again she tried to pull the trigger. *Please help me.... Please...*

COLE WORKED frantically to pry open the shields. The power surge had closed them completely. No one knew why the electricity suspended itself in the mountains west of Phoenix when storms moved over the valley. It was just another bewildering weather phenomenon peculiar to the geography.

He'd almost missed the call, the one from the pathologist giving him the results of the blood work Kate had requested earlier that evening. He had tried calling her. When there was no answer, instinct told him where to find her.

Pelting rain soaked him. Occasionally, bolts of lightning lit up the entire area. With the sunshields down, the only way into the house was through the bathroom window. He prayed for it to be unlocked. The pane easily slid open for him to enter. He snaked his way through, into the tub. Only then did he draw his weapon.

Like a cat, he inched his way down the long hallway. Familiar voices floated ahead of him. *Stay alive, Kate!* It was hot inside the house. And in the still, humid air, smell traveled with the same clarity as sound. Traces of Kate's soft fragrance reached him.

Sweat trickled down the back of his neck. Fear oozed through him—not for himself, but for Kate. He hoped she would spot him before he startled her into firing at him. And if she fired, so would Libby. All he could think about was getting his hand around Kate's mouth and lifting her backward out of the line of fire.

Faster.

His eyes were adjusting, and he couldn't see Kate. The realization jerked at his panic, releasing it, tightening it again. He felt along the wall in the hallway, until his hand grazed the handle of the breaker box.

A brief sound of movement caught his attention, and he whirled toward the kitchen to face a bright, deafening explosion. At once another shot exploded so close to his head, Cole heard its passage.

"No-o-o!" a voice cried. His voice. By the time he had the lights on, Kate lay crumpled on the kitchen floor. For an instant, the hot agony of fear gripped him. Paralyzed him.

"She shouldn't have interfered," Libby was muttering.

In the next instant, he whirled to face the only mother he'd ever known, seeking madness in her eyes, seeing nothing but despair. She had the gun pointed to her head. If she so much as touched the trigger, she would die.

"No!" he yelled, but the c-l-i-c-k drowned out his plea.

KATE FELT HERSELF falling back as if in slow motion, back on her heels, back even farther until her legs slipped out from under her. Her spine sank onto the floor, and her head followed. It seemed she could hear her body sighing.

Her head burned now. The skin there felt sticky and wet. She wanted to sit up, but couldn't. She wasn't certain she could move. Now Cole was leaning very close to her, so close she could smell the gunsmoke in his hair. She opened her mouth to say something, then closed it again. Tears dropped onto her cheeks. His tears.

Distantly, she heard weeping. Still she couldn't say anything. She could only lie there while her body was mysteriously weighted to the floor. Then his hand was stroking her face, brushing away the tears. She was no longer afraid. *Safe.* She knew she was safe. Cole's arms closed around her. When she touched a hand to his cheek, he pressed his forehead against hers.

"You came," she said in a wondering voice.

"It's okay, it's okay," he whispered, holding her, rocking her.

Reality sank in. She was alive because of Cole. He had helped rescue her, and he hadn't let her down.

"Stay alive, babe. For me," he was murmuring.

The easy endearment made her heart twist. Emotion clogged her throat. Was he trying to tell her he was still in love with her? That he wouldn't let her go this time?

"No problem," she told him, because there was too much at stake to die now. She just might have a future, after all.

Chapter Eighteen

Cole didn't bother to turn on the lights in his apartment. He moved about by rote, eventually ending up in the living room, collapsing on the sofa. Kate had suffered a superficial wound to the head. The bullet had only grazed her. After extensive tests, the emergency-room doctor had decided to keep her overnight for observation. No one had been seriously wounded*...physically.*

Libby had emptied her gun by the time she had turned it on herself. She had not uttered a coherent word since. She was being kept in the maximum-security unit at the state hospital for the mentally insane. Cole had visited, but she didn't recognize him.

The mayor had refused his resignation. More political machinations, Cole assumed. He'd taken a leave of absence from his job. His future now seemed more uncertain than his troubled past.

Maybe Kate had been right. He had to look within himself, listen to his own heart. Maybe the time had come for him to leave this dark phase of his life behind.

There was only one place to accomplish that. Wickenburg. Home. Where he'd put down roots. Where he'd first found love....

KATE HAD WAITED THREE hours in the emergency room to spend three minutes with a busy doctor who concluded that her injuries were superficial. She'd been shipped off to spend the night in a hospital room. For observation, the busy doctor had said. For thinking and sorting, Kate had thought, as Cole walked away. And all too quickly inspiration came. At this crucial moment in her life, Kate realized she wasn't longing for her mother and father any longer, or her next assignment with the Bureau; she wanted Cole—the only person in the world who had the power to ease the pain in her heart. And in a poignant choice between his mother and her, Cole had chosen Kate. His act of courage was the epitome of trust. But now he was gone—out of her life—maybe forever.

Nurses shuttled in and out of her room all night, making it impossible for her to sleep—even if she could have. A message from the Bureau chief had said, "Well done. Take some time off. But not too much." Kate laughed. She was beginning to heal. There were numerous vapid telephone messages from the mayor who wanted personally to tell Kate he was her strongest supporter; that he'd had faith in her judgment all along.

At the first sign of daylight, Kate called for a nurse. She had to get out of here. In her heart she was still so weighted with pain, she wasn't certain she could stand.

A uniformed aide appeared to help her out of bed to dress.

As she walked outside into the sunshine, she gained momentum. She had to match Cole's courage. He hadn't let her down. She needed to thank him . . . and much more.

BACK IN WICKENBURG, Cole strolled the nature path to the river's edge. Things were all too clear to him now. The answers had been right there inside him all along. In his heart.

"Hi," Kate said softly.

The landscape, with the river slicing through the desert hills, blurred. The sun glinting off the charming red-tiled roofs and whitewashed buildings went unnoticed. Only the sight of Kate's dark head and the proud set of her shoulders was real to him.

"Hi," he murmured, trying to slow the beat of his heart. "You okay?"

"Yes." She nodded. "I wasn't certain you'd be here."

"I thought you would be on your way back to Quantico."

Seeing her stirred something inside him, making it hard to keep his mind on business. He wondered why she'd returned. He looked out over the river again.

"I keep telling myself the solution is to sell the place."

He felt her start. "I don't know, Cole. Maybe you're rushing things."

They exchanged another glance.

He couldn't tell whether it was really the place that concerned her, or the idea of losing all the wonderful memories. Maybe he didn't know himself.

"The Judge used to walk me down to the riverbank—to this very spot—when I was a kid. We'd talk about everything. He'd often talk to me about the gift of life, about being honest with yourself if you were ever to be really happy. I thought he meant something else—something on the order of knowing who you really were."

"The only thing he was guilty of," Kate said gently, "was refusing to acknowledge Libby's deteriorating condition from her drinking." She paused to study him. "She knew there was never an affair."

He nodded.

"Winter would probably draw a better price," Kate said, returning to the most innocuous topic.

"Probably."

"We'd miss this place."

We? He wondered if it was significant. Or was he just reading something into her words? All he wanted was to touch her, to reach out and pull her into his arms and know that her love belonged to him and him alone—not for just tonight, but from now on.

"Kate..."

She turned to face him.

"I have to know something," he said.

"Took you long enough."

"Why did you come?"

"I had to know something, too," she breathed, feeling afraid and hopeful at the same time.

"Come here."

She was in his arms in a heartbeat, tilting her chin up to him.

"Nothing's changed," he murmured.

"That's good," she said. "We were in love the last time I thought about it. Sounds like a good enough reason to me for us to be together, to make our own family." She paused and bit at her lower lip. "Libby told me everything."

"Did she tell you that I was abandoned as a child—that I don't have a clue where I came from—or from whom?"

"Did you think it would matter?"

She gazed up at him, her warm brown eyes melting. He framed her face with his hands, stroking back her hair.

"At one time, it stood in the way of everything. The whole idea of not knowing about my beginnings—made me feel different."

"But the McGuires were wonderful parents."

"That's just it. I loved and trusted them, yet the mother who adopted me was a—"

"I know," Kate said with compassion in her voice.

"I did a lot of thinking last night, Kate. I realized that life is all about what's *inside* you. It's not a matter of upbringing, but of how you live your life."

"I know that now," she agreed. "I've been trying to substitute my job for my family, when I should have been building my own life. That's what happiness is all about. You're right. It's what we make of our lives. And," she added, "you'll make a wonderful father."

"You think so?" He felt his eyes light up, his heart lift.

"Of course, we don't want to rush into anything—just one baby at a time."

He smiled.

They had survived this; everything else would be easy.

"Come here," he murmured. "I want you close when I tell you how much I love you."

INDULGE A LITTLE 6947 SWEEPSTAKES
NO PURCHASE NECESSARY

HERE'S HOW THE SWEEPSTAKES WORKS:
The Harlequin Reader Service shipments for January, February and March 1994 will contain, respectively, coupons for entry into three prize drawings: a trip for two to San Francisco, an Alaskan cruise for two and a trip for two to Hawaii. To be eligible for any drawing using an Entry Coupon, simply complete and mail according to directions.

There is no obligation to continue as a Reader Service subscriber to enter and be eligible for any prize drawing. You may also enter any drawing by hand printing your name and address on a 3" x 5" card and the destination of the prize you wish that entry to be considered for (i.e., San Francisco trip, Alaskan cruise or Hawaiian trip). Send your 3" x 5" entries to: Indulge a Little 6947 Sweepstakes, c/o Prize Destination you wish that entry to be considered for, P.O. Box 1315, Buffalo, NY 14269-1315, U.S.A. or Indulge a Little 6947 Sweepstakes, P.O. Box 610, Fort Erie, Ontario L2A 5X3, Canada.

To be eligible for the San Francisco trip, entries must be received by 4/30/94; for the Alaskan cruise, 5/31/94; and the Hawaiian trip, 6/30/94. No responsibility is assumed for lost, late or misdirected mail. Sweepstakes open to residents of the U.S. (except Puerto Rico) and Canada, 18 years of age or older. All applicable laws and regulations apply. Sweepstakes void wherever prohibited.

For a copy of the Official Rules, send a self-addressed, stamped envelope (WA residents need not affix return postage) to: Indulge a Little 6947 Rules, P.O. Box 4631, Blair, NE 68009, U.S.A.

INDR93

INDULGE A LITTLE 6947 SWEEPSTAKES
NO PURCHASE NECESSARY

HERE'S HOW THE SWEEPSTAKES WORKS:
The Harlequin Reader Service shipments for January, February and March 1994 will contain, respectively, coupons for entry into three prize drawings: a trip for two to San Francisco, an Alaskan cruise for two and a trip for two to Hawaii. To be eligible for any drawing using an Entry Coupon, simply complete and mail according to directions.

There is no obligation to continue as a Reader Service subscriber to enter and be eligible for any prize drawing. You may also enter any drawing by hand printing your name and address on a 3" x 5" card and the destination of the prize you wish that entry to be considered for (i.e., San Francisco trip, Alaskan cruise or Hawaiian trip). Send your 3" x 5" entries to: Indulge a Little 6947 Sweepstakes, c/o Prize Destination you wish that entry to be considered for, P.O. Box 1315, Buffalo, NY 14269-1315, U.S.A. or Indulge a Little 6947 Sweepstakes, P.O. Box 610, Fort Erie, Ontario L2A 5X3, Canada.

To be eligible for the San Francisco trip, entries must be received by 4/30/94; for the Alaskan cruise, 5/31/94; and the Hawaiian trip, 6/30/94. No responsibility is assumed for lost, late or misdirected mail. Sweepstakes open to residents of the U.S. (except Puerto Rico) and Canada, 18 years of age or older. All applicable laws and regulations apply. Sweepstakes void wherever prohibited.

For a copy of the Official Rules, send a self-addressed, stamped envelope (WA residents need not affix return postage) to: Indulge a Little 6947 Rules, P.O. Box 4631, Blair, NE 68009, U.S.A.

INDR93

INDULGE A LITTLE SWEEPSTAKES

OFFICIAL ENTRY COUPON

This entry must be received by: MAY 31, 1994
This month's winner will be notified by: JUNE 15, 1994
Trip must be taken between: JULY 31, 1994-JULY 31, 1995

YES, I want to win the Alaskan Cruise vacation for two. I understand that the prize includes round-trip airfare, one-week cruise including private cabin, all meals and pocket money as revealed on the "wallet" scratch-off card.

Name______________________________

Address____________________ Apt.__________

City______________________________

State/Prov.________________ Zip/Postal Code__________

Daytime phone number________________________
(Area Code)

Account #______________________________

Return entries with invoice in envelope provided. Each book in this shipment has two entry coupons—and the more coupons you enter, the better your chances of winning!

 MONTH2

INDULGE A LITTLE SWEEPSTAKES

OFFICIAL ENTRY COUPON

This entry must be received by: MAY 31, 1994
This month's winner will be notified by: JUNE 15, 1994
Trip must be taken between: JULY 31, 1994-JULY 31, 1995

YES, I want to win the Alaskan Cruise vacation for two. I understand that the prize includes round-trip airfare, one-week cruise including private cabin, all meals and pocket money as revealed on the "wallet" scratch-off card.

Name______________________________

Address____________________ Apt.__________

City______________________________

State/Prov.________________ Zip/Postal Code__________

Daytime phone number________________________
(Area Code)

Account #______________________________

Return entries with invoice in envelope provided. Each book in this shipment has two entry coupons—and the more coupons you enter, the better your chances of winning!

© 1993 HARLEQUIN ENTERPRISES LTD. MONTH2